WATERS OF CREATION

WATERS OF CREATION

Marilyn J. Masten

Copyright © 1998 by Marilyn J. Masten.

Library of Congress Number	98-85955
ISBN (Hardcover)	0-7388-0000-7
(Softcover)	0-7388-0032-5

All rights reserved. No part of this book may be reproduced or transmitted in any form or by any means, electronic or mechanical, including photocopying, recording, or by any information storage and retrieval system, without permission in writing from the copyright owner.

This is a work of fiction. Names, characters, places and incidents either are the product of the author's imagination or are used fictitiously, and any resemblance to any actual persons, living or dead, events, or locales is entirely coincidental.

This book was printed in the United States of America.

To order additional copies of this book, contact:
Xlibris Corporation
PO Box 2199
Princeton, NJ 08543-2199
USA

1-888-7-XLIBRIS
1-609-278-0075
www.Xlibris.com
Orders@Xlibris.com

CONTENTS

INTRODUCTION 9
Chapter 1 13
Chapter 2 36
Chapter 3 55
Chapter 4 80
Chapter 5 95
Chapter 6 116
Chapter 7 136

FOR THE WATERS OF CREATION AND THE PEOPLE OF CLEVELAND WHOSE SPIRIT IS AS THE GREAT LAKE SHE SITS BESIDE; FOR THEY ARE AS THE "WILDCAT", SYNOMYMOUS WITH THE "ERIE TRIBE AND BRETHERN TO THE MIGHTY IROQUOIS NATION."

SPECIAL THANKS TO MY PARENTS, JOE AND JEAN, MY SISTER, JOANN, AND THE "APOLLO OF DOGS".

INTRODUCTION

Six years have passed since China's human wave of war upon the World has finally ended. Death and destruction engulfed the entire world during this time and now nature, and what is left of humanity, is on a course of a slow and agonizing death. Few nations survive, and those that do must now endure the magnitude of cataclysm suffered by all of creation as the earth and its land masses have physically changed. Not one corner of the world remained untouched as former countries and whole continents have become almost unfamiliar. South America has ruptured from her Sister to the North, while Europe's ground cracks and breaks as it trembles in fear from quakes and volcanic eruptions, spewing red lava into her once sparkling Blue Mediterranean Sea. The Mountain Ranges of the Earth revolt in anger, violently shaking and filling the skies with unequaled volumes of dirt and debris that have changed their magnificent faces forever. Although the land mass of North America remains somewhat intact, nearly 3/4 of her population have been annilated, for millions have perished; and remnants of once favored cities are scattered in ruin with mankind huddled together like children still living in a nightmare of terror. Beguiled by the evil entity, China's brutal leaders were promised great power over the world, and so led the Yellow Race into believing they would rule the earth above all others; but they too have suffered unimaginable and enormous loss of life, so that China now has only two million left within her lost boundaries. Through wars, corruption, and greed, mankind has all but destroyed his environment, and what is left of man is now homeless; living in streets, rat infested alleys, and crumbling buildings; for thirst, hunger, squalor, and fear are the diseases of this new Earth. Many lush plants and trees no longer exist except for sparse desert vegetation and these too will soon wither, as nature dearly clings to life knowing full well the end is near; For the earth's atmosphere is polluted and with each year that passes, the altered sun grows stronger as it sends its sweltering rays to the earth's surface. The once mighty seas, lakes, and rivers are slowly becoming craters of death as the merciless sun star relentlessly evaporates Earth's waters into dust bowls of extinction. No birds are to be seen flying or singing praises to the Heavens, for there are no clouds, no rain or winds to carry their wings,and the Four Seasons are but a long, lost memory. Trillions of brilliant gem-stars that once glittered in the evening sky can no longer be seen, for the shade of night does not exist and Earth's moon now belongs to the planet, Mars. The days of praying and hoping that modern technology, science, and the age of computers would save them is over, for only a miracle can save mankind from the cruel destiny of the surging endless day where the agony of evil still prevails. It has been written that the evil one has waged many battles against God and humanity since the beginnings of creation, and Satan celebrates for he has gathered many souls since the birth of creation; but still he is not satisfied, as The Holy Waters are the key to which Satan vows dominion over all that was created by Almighty God. And so in this year of 2039, a great battle is destined to take place between Archangel and the Fallen Angel for the

WATERS OF CREATION

CHAPTER 1

Few cities of the earth and in the land of freedom survive, holding on to the past; not knowing if there will be a future for mankind. In the once vibrant city of Cleveland, Felicia and her grand-daughter Angella lived in a somewhat sheltered parking lot overlooking Lake Erie; herself known as one of five Great Lakes linked together in natural wonder. Like the others, she was a beautiful fresh-water lake who could be gentle, serene, and even kind at times; but unlike the others, her waters were the shallowest and the most treacherous as her temperament could turn in an instant with a show of her powerful force and endurance to fight whomever dared conquer her; for she was queen and master of this region with an indomitable will of her own. Those that lived upon her shores would have to learn to live beside her and not against her, or they would surely feel the wrath of her fury as she is the "Wildcat", synonymous with the "Erie Tribe" and brethren to the Mighty Iroquois Nation. Many centuries have now passed and the people who lived on her shores and in her closely knit villages, became as one with the Great Cat, for they had taken on and mirrored her strength and tenacious personality. They worked hard and fought for what they believed in to the very end no matter what the outcome; but now the She-Cat grows weak; no longer looking strong and healthy, and as each year, month, and day passes, she recedes more and more from her shrinking edges, drying up and slowly dying just as her people. Felicia was in her mid forties, with dark brown and lustrous hair with a slight hint of graying at her temples, but even in her tattered slacks and rumpled shirt-waist blouse, she had a quality of inner beauty and nobility about her, while at the same time, she was a loving and caring person devoted to her grand-daughter. However, living in this hostile climate was taking its toll on her physically and mentally, but she knew she had to stay strong for Angella's sake. There was still much Angella needed to learn and Felicia thanked God that He had kept her strong enough to be a survivor. As Felicia looked at her dozing Grand-daughter, She began thinking of the little girl's parents who had survived the horror of war only to die from a fatal virus a couple of years before. As she wiped a tear from her cheek, she thought back to when she, herself, was a little girl and how the city had been such a wonderful and exciting place to be, for life was so very good then. She remembered the baseball and football games her parents took her to, the All American hot dogs that were eaten on 4th of July picnics, and all of the fun their family had once known. As her mind wandered through the past, she reminisced over her school days, the dances she enjoyed as a teenager, her first date, finally meeting the man of her dreams, and how life was so complete without care or fear of what the future held. She came back to reality and looked toward the Rock and Roll Hall of Fame, a once stellar palace of honor, shaped in the form of a magnificent and slanted/glass Triangle that towered and glistened on the very edge of Lake Erie. But now in this year of 2039, many of its sparkling crystal windows that captured the beams of moonlight and music were now shattered or broken, with just a few remaining intact. Felicia fixed her gaze upon the lake and thought of the Four Season weather that she had remembered while growing up in this North Coast City known for its harsh winters. She inhaled very softly and slowly as if savoring every image and smell that Indian Summer and Fall brought to her mind when the beautiful maple trees turned their leaves to brilliant, golden-yellow and orange colors that once dotted the countryside. She then closed her eyes gently, hoping to remember the cold feeling of winter's wind-blown snowflakes descending from heaven and touching her face. As her eyes opened, she thought that all she had left were these special memories and hoped their vision and sensation would always stay vivid in her mind. Felicia gazed upon Angella's face and felt sadness in her heart, for she realized that at least she had many wonderful memories; but Angella had never seen or felt what she had experienced. "Oh God, Help us". "My grand-daughter will never know what I have known".

"None of the children will ever know, see, or feel what I have seen, and none of them will ever have such wonderful memories of nature and what the world was truly like then".

As Angella rubbed her eyes, Felicia tried to wipe the tears from her own eyes before Angella would notice that she had been crying.

"Grand mama. Were you dreaming again?"

As Felicia began to answer Angella, she smiled; for Angella was an adorable little girl who looked just as her name sounded. She was a beautiful little angel of a child with soft, curly blonde locks of hair, cute plump dimples, and big round laughter-filled eyes; and she was eager to learn everything she could from her grandmother.

Felicia answered Angella's questioning eyes

"I guess I can't keep any secrets from you, now can I"?

"Grandma, are you really going to tell me a special story for my birthday, like you promised"?, asked Angella.

"Why of course dear; "my goodness, you'll be 7 years old tomorrow, and I promise it will be a birthday you'll never forget",

And as Felicia spoke these words, little did she realize how prophetic they would be.

"Grandma, I just know that you, Sam, and me will have a lot of fun tomorrow".

At the mention of Sam's name, Felicia realized that Sam had been gone a little too long and this made her uncomfortable knowing what could happen to a 13 year old boy out on the streets. There were plenty of good people left, but there were still some very bad people out there just waiting to prey on the weak, young, and the old. Even though she hoped Sam could take care of himself, he did have some sort of facial paralysis and because of this, he had to be careful because people tried to take advantage of him.

Sam's parents also lived in the parking lot beside Felicia and her family. His father was Apache Indian and his mother was French and from this beautiful combination, Sam's heritage could be seen with his thick jet black hair, high cheek bones denoting his Apache Indian ancestry, and a fine featured face with large, dark-brown eyes. It was a pity that the boy had a partially crooked face. Before the war, Sam's father, Billy, worked on the repair of the many colorfully lit bridges that sit at the edge of the lake, the Cuyahoga River, and at the foot of the city. Sam's mother also died from the same virus a few weeks after Angella's parents had passed away, and Billy had been devastated by his wife's death. He went into a deep state of depression and walked to one of the tallest bridges that he had previously worked on, and climbed the bridge very sure footed, just as a true Apache warrior once climbed mountains so very long ago to pray to his God; and when Billy just about reached the very top of the bridge, he accidentally slipped and fell. Later that day, a citizen on patrol came and told Felicia what had happened. Miraculously, Billy was still alive, however, he had sustained significant brain damage and would be a paraplegic. He had been brought to the downtown make-shift hospital where he had been kept there until there was nothing more they could do for him. Felicia felt very sorry for Billy, and especially for the boy, Sam; and so she took care of them as if they were part of her own family. Usually, a group of them would go to the Great Hall Building to pick up their monthly allotment of food tickets while Carl, a senior citizen, would watch Billy. This time, though, Sam had insisted on going alone and even refused to take Chief, a huge, lumbering Great Dane, along with him. A couple of days after his father's tragic accident, Sam found the hurt pup dying in the street, so he brought the dog home and begged Felicia to let him keep the animal. At first she was against the idea, but then feeling guilty, she finally relented and allowed Sam to keep the dog. Even though this was against her better judgment, Felicia felt that Sam and Angella deserved a little happiness as children, however she made them promise that if food and drinking-water were to become more rationed in the future, the dog would then have to go. To Felicia's surprise, Chief grew into a magnificently powerful animal with great size, beautiful fawn color, and an outstanding black mask that enveloped his large nose and flues that set him apart. He truly commanded respect with a head and paws that were absolutely massive and a tail that was long and heavy with a whip-like action. Felicia was wondering if she had made the right decision, although she did have to admit that he was a terrific gentle companion to the children and she did feel safer when they all slept, for Chief would guard them with his life. As a matter of fact, many of the other families appreciated Chief too as they all contributed tidbits for him when they could, for they also felt protected and viewed him as their community watch dog. As each minute passed, Felicia became more uneasy, feeling worried that something had happened to Sam. She thought to herself; what if someone hurt him to get extra food tickets; then she would never forgive herself. At that moment, Byron, a tall and very muscular, black teenage boy of about 16, could be seen leaving the underground parking lot. He was a tough but quiet kid who lived in the parking lot with his parents, Sara and Joe. Sara had a heart of gold and tried her best to look after the elderly and sick people who also lived in their parking lot community. Felicia admired Sara and marveled at her beautiful singing voice that could be softly heard resonating throughout the parking lot, lulling everyone's worries to sleep. Felicia had been a teacher before the War and had gotten to know many of the families as she taught the younger children as much as she could. Because of the age of computers, books had become obsolete in the classroom; but since Felicia had no access to computers, let alone electricity and hook-ups for themselves, she relied on some of her personal books which she had managed to salvage after the War. And, so she did the best she could with the hope of at least teaching the young children how to read and write. Sara would occasionally come by and listen as Felicia taught the youngsters, and this warmed Sara's heart as it made her think of her own childhood days. They soon developed a loving friendship and together, they reminisced about their lives before the war and what would become of them now. Felicia waved to Byron, hoping to get his attention before he left, and as he approached, she asked him.

"Byron, are you going in the direction of the Great Hall"?
As Byron came toward her, he replied.
"Yeah..Felicia, Why?".
In a concerned voice, she asked,
"Please, Byron, Please do me a favor."
"I'm pretty worried about Sam because he went there a few hours ago and he's still not back".
"Do you think you could look for him?"
Byron knew that Felicia must really be worried because she had never asked him for any favors.
"Sure...Felicia". If I see him, I'll tell him to get home quick",
And as Byron walked out of the parking lot, Chief followed him.

After waiting in line for an hour, Sam finally received the portion of tickets for the month's food allotment and smiled politely at the clerk. As he left the clerk's window, he counted the coupons and put them in his shirt pocket, not realizing that he was being watched by three teenage boys who had noticed his crooked-looking face and figured he would be very easy prey. As Sam happily walked out of the Great Building, the group of teenagers walked a distance behind him waiting for the right time to strike.

Sam stopped at the opening of an alley where an old man weakly motioned to him.

"Boy, Boy, Don't be Afraid."

Sam hesitated and was about to keep on walking, but the old man softly insisted that he would not hurt Sam, and in a sincere and pleading voice,

"I'm too old to hurt anyone, boy". "I have some extra food tickets if you want them".

"I won't be needing them anymore and from the looks of you, you could sure use them".

Sam looked down at the pavement and then back to the old man, as he accepted the food coupons.

"Thank You, Sir".

"My family will appreciate these very much, but are you sure you won't need them"?

The man then nodded his head as he answered,

"Yes, I'm very sure". "Just go on home now and may God be with you".

The three teenagers who had been stalking Sam, quietly watched and smiled at each other, confirming Sam would be their next victim, for they were confident they would be feasting for many weeks to come. Sam was about 1 block away from home now, and as he passed another alley, the three boys grabbed him and began to push him around while demanding all of the food tickets. They told him that they would disfigure the other side of his face if they didn't get them. There was no way out of the alley and Sam didn't know how he was going to get out of this as the three boys came toward him with switch blades. Suddenly, Chief's deep, low growl was heard as he stood at Byron's side as he readied himself to attack. Byron and Sam never really talked to each other, but there was kind of an unspoken thing between them. Nobody messed with Byron and almost everyone in the area knew who he was, including the three teenage boys. Even though he and Sam were not close buddies, Byron watched out for Sam because he felt sort of sorry for Sam and his dad, but Byron was the type of guy who would never admit to that sort of sentiment, nor would he ever think of hanging around with someone younger than he was. After all, Byron had a tough image to uphold in the neighborhood, but nobody was going to mess with any of the people that lived in his parking lot, not to mention the fact that Felicia had personally asked him to look for Sam.!! As Byron ran toward two of the teenagers, Chief leaped toward the other teen and with all of the force of his weight, he knocked the youth up against a brick wall. He continually snarled and growled as he kept the teenager pinned against the wall, daring him to move, while Byron handled the other two teens as if they were toys and gave them a lesson in street fighting.

After Byron was finished, Chief released the other boy from the wall and all three of them finally ran off down the street. Sam was surprised that Byron had helped him, but yet Sam really didn't want to admit that he was scared.

"Thank's Byron, but I probably could have taken care of myself".

Byron looked at Sam and laughed.

"Kid..You're not such a good liar."

"You were shakin like a baby".

"Just be thankful me and your dog saved your little ass".

Sam momentarily paused as he looked at Byron and then took out the extra food tickets the old man had given him and handed them to Byron.

"Here, you deserve these".

Byron was too proud to accept anything, especially from a 13 year old!!!.

"No Man, I'm no sissy" .

"No Way" "Just go home, Sam".

"Felicia is pretty upset wondering if you're okay, so you better run all the way like a real Apache."

"Oh, and do me a favor, don't tell nobody what I did here today".

"I gotta go now kid. "See ya later".

Sam put the tickets back in his pocket and stooped down to hug and thank Chief. Felicia and Angella were getting ready to look for Sam when Felicia heard someone running on the roof of the parking lot above. As Sam ran into their level of the parking lot, she could hear that his voice was filled with excitement.

"Felicia....Felicia"., he yelled as he ran toward her.

Felicia sighed with relief at seeing Sam.

"I was so worried about you".

"I'm okay, I'm okay, guess What Felicia"? "I got extra food tickets, I got extra food tickets", Sam excitedly stated.

Felicia looked around hoping none of the other families that were huddled together in different parts of the parking shelter would hear what Sam was saying.

"Sh" "Sh, Quiet Sam." "Not so loud" "What Happened"?

Lowering his voice, Sam began to tell Felicia and Angella how a very old man came up to him and handed him the extra food tickets, telling him that he wouldn't be needing them anymore. There was a moment of silence as Felicia's and Sam's eyes met, for she knew what had happend. Many of the very elderly felt hopeless in that they had lived their lives with no reason to live on, only taking up space and food that the young needed more than they, and so a lot of them committed suicide by starving in order that the younger population could live on. It was a very sad situation, but a fact of life in the year 2039 on earth. Felicia took Sam and Angella by their hands as they knealt to say a prayer for the old man who had given Sam the food coupons. Billy, Sam's father, sat propped up against the wall in the underground parking lot, just staring out into space as Felicia and the children prayed.

"Dear God", Please have mercy on the man who gave us his portion of food".

"Be kind and gentle to him, dear Lord".

As both children answered "Amen", Felicia decided that she would give the food tickets to Father Vincent, for he would know of a needy family that could use them. Sam stood up and looked around the huge underground parking lot.

"Where's Chief?"

"He was right behind me when I ran into the parking lot"

"Where did he go now?"

Out of nowhere, and running at full speed, Chief playfully bounded straight toward Sam with something in his mouth while trying to bark at the same time. Somewhere, somehow, he had found a ball and wanted to play catch with Sam and Angella as he often did, but this time the children laughed hysterically at the site of Chief who looked so awkward as he pranced, danced, and snorted. Felicia tried to contain her own laughter but couldn't because the site of him reminded her of a reindeer who was getting ready to pull Santa's sleigh, and all Chief needed was a pair of Antlers. They roared with laughter, but Billy didn't bat an eyelash for he seemed oblivious to everything around him. As Felicia glanced at Billy, she told the kids they had all had enough excitement for the day, when Sam suddenly noticed Byron walk into the parking lot. Byron momentarily hesitated as Sam and he looked at each other for a brief second, just long enough for Byron to notice the look of appreciation on Sam's face. And then a half-smile crossed Byron's lips as he turned and went to the other side of the parking lot to join his family. Even though the sun was hot and bright, it was time to get some rest and Felicia wanted to get up early the next morning.

"Tomorrow is a very special day"

" We're all going to have a wonderful time celebrating Angella's birthday, so lets all get some rest now."

Angella and Sam got into their make-shift beds as Chief took his usual place between them and rested his head on Sam's leg. Felicia checked on Billy and then glanced over at the children as she thought about Angella's birthday tomorrow, wishing that she could give her grand-daughter a real birthday party like she had when she was a child. Felicia felt completely helpless and to her, it seemed so sad that Angella or Sam would ever experience the wonderful things in life that she had taken for granted when she was young and growing up. She never dreamed in a million years that life would be like this for not only her own grand-daughter, but for so many other children. Felicia thought about the death of Sam's mother and of her own daughter and son-in-law, and she thought about St. John's Cathedral and how they had been designated to use their food coupons at the great church which was only a few blocks from the parking lot. The cathedral was one of the safest places to be and even though the food tickets allowed them only one meal per day, they were very grateful, for it was enough to keep them from starving. Since they had been obtaining their meals at the Cathedral now for the past 2 years, Felicia had hoped she could move all of them into the Cathedral to live. She was not getting any younger and didn't know how much longer she could take care of the children and Billy by herself. She knew she would feel more secure if she could only get them off of the streets and into the safety of the Church. Father Vincent put her on the list because of Billy's condition, but she knew the wait would be long, for everyone wanted to move into the Cathedral for better living conditions and safety. Orphans, young families with children under 4 years of age, and pregnant woman had first priority, followed by all other families according to priorities of health, age, and special circumstances. As she closed her eyes, Felicia could hear Sara's sweet melody in the distance and Felicia thought to herself that she would make it a point to talk to Father Vincent tomorrow and hoped they would not have to wait much longer to move into the Cathedral.

The sun's rays were extremely hot and dry as they spread to the earth below, making it uncomfortably warm in the, somewhat, sheltered parking lot, but at least there was a small sanctuary of shade, as Felicia tied her hair back with a long piece of tattered cloth. Today would be a day of happiness and celebration for Angella's 7th birthday had arrived and Felicia finished brushing Angella's curls while Sam patiently prepared Billy for their trip to the Cathedral. Sam wiped the sweat from his father's face, and as always, carried on a conversation with his dad, even though he wasn't sure that Billy even understood anything that he was saying.

"Dad, you're going to enjoy today cause we're going to the Church for our meal and to celebrate Angella's birthday".

Angella laughed and joined in the conversation..

"Yes, Billy, I'm 7 years old today and Grandmama says I'm not a little baby anymore".

"I'm getting all grown up now".

Turning to Felicia, Angella asked about the special story that Felicia promised to tell them.

"Grandma, when are we going to hear the story?"

Laughing, Felicia answered her,

"I'm going to save the best for last, but first we'll enjoy the whole day together as a family and when we return, I promise you sweet dreams with a wonderful story of a secret Paradise."

Angella responded with a giggle and Sam smiled broadly as he finished getting his father ready for the trip. Just as Sam finished, Byron's family approached Felicia. They usually joined Felicia's family to walk to the Cathedral, for they also took their meals at the same church, but it was really more than that. They had all become good friends and quite frankly, there was safety in number when walking the few blocks en route to the Cathedral. Byron always joined them on Sunday and usually walked behind everyone as if he were keeping watch while the rest of the group walked ahead. Sara's husband, Joe, was a strapping man of about 6'2", muscularly built who worked in construction along with many of the other men to help rebuild the city; and he, like Sara, could always be counted on to help out whenever he was needed. Byron stood to one side, quiet and aloof, as his parents greeted Felicia and the two children. Joe then asked Byron to help lift Billy into the dilapidated, but trusty, old wheelchair that Father Vincent had donated to Felicia. As they walked to Church, Felicia and Sara talked incessantly, oblivious to everything around them, while Angella skipped happily at their sides. Every now and then, Joe would put his hand on Billy's shoulder, reassuring Billy that everything was fine while he continued pushing the wheelchair. Sam walked beside his father as Chief pranced to the rhythm of the rolling wheels and every so often, Sam would look over his shoulder to see if Byron was still behind them. He wished Byron would stop treating him like a kid because he was not a child anymore, for many hundreds of years ago, he would have been a young warrior by now, according to the Apache tradition of manhood. Sam decided to take the initiative and stopped to wait for Byron to catch up. Byron looked at him, but seemed a little embarrassed hoping that no-one else would see that Sam was waiting to walk with him. Because of Sam's facial paralysis, he often had problems making people understand what he was trying to say and most people were impatient and made fun of his speech. Felicia and Angella were the only two people in the world that really took the time to understand Sam and give him a chance to say what was on his mind without laughing at him. Sam also had a very special secret that only he and Chief shared, for all he had to do would be to look at his dog and think about the words he wanted to say to his great friend, and Chief understood even before Sam could get one word out. He and Chief had that special bond just as the Apache had with his horse so many hundreds of years ago. As Byron approached, he looked at Sam out of the corner of his eye, wondering why Sam had decided to wait for him. Sam stumbled with forced but sincere words.

"No...No....matter" "No matter whaa what you might think of me, I'm not a baby any anymore",

Byron took a deep breath but said nothing. Sam was a little surprised that Byron seemed to let him talk without interrupting him.

"I really did ap apre appreciate your help that day", Sam confided.

Byron looked straight ahead as he finally answered.

"Right Sam, but you're still a kid and you proved it that day" "You could uv never fought those guys off alone". "They would uv killed you over them food tickets."

Still stammering, Sam said

"O..Okay". "Then teach me"

"Teach me how to fight".

The words came easier now and Sam felt more comfortable talking to Byron as he felt the ice had finally been broken between them.

Byron laughed as he repeated Sam's words....

"Teach me?" "I can't teach you".

"It's something that comes natural, Kid".

Sam held his head high with confidence.

"I'm an Apache Warrior with no Warrior to show me the Way

to manhood"

"My father cannot show me now".

"You must show me."

A look of surprise crossed Byron's face as he heard Sam's words and answered him.

"Sam, I'm not Apache", Byron answered.

"How can I show you the Apache Way?"

"I mean show me how to fight", Sam stated loud and clear without a hint of a speech defect.

Byron raised his eyebrows and his eyes widened as he stopped and placed his hand on Sam's shoulder; and with a pause that seemed to be an eternity, looked into Sam's pleading, but determined eyes.

"Okay. Okay Kid, I'll teach you".

For the first time, Sam felt accepted by someone that he looked up to like a brother, and from that moment on, Sam knew that this was the beginning of a true and lasting friendship. The group approached the Cathedral and Chief began panting with excitement for this was his favorite place, as he associated the Cathedral with food because of the many tidbits he received. As everyone stood before the great steps leading into the Church, Chief ran near a side entrance where he had previously dug a large, but shallow, hole to hide some of his booty and also keep cool in the dirt while he waited patiently for his master's return with more treats for him. The Great Cathedral was always filled to capacity on Sunday; all waiting for Father Vincent to begin the Mass as was the custom before the meal was served in the Great Banquet Hall beneath the Church. Since many great temples and houses of worship had been destroyed with only a few left intact, Father Vincent shared his Church with Rabbi Silverman, Father Thomas of the Greek Faith, and Pastor Bennett, an Episcopalian. Each of them lived in the Parish house with Father Vincent and each shared in the use of the Cathedral in order to hold services for their religious faithful, and because of this, Father Vincent was highly admired and respected. Over the years, they had all become very good friends as they worked together, became more tolerant of each other's beliefs, and often consulted each other in making decisions that ultimately would affect the combined congregation. The interior of St. John's had been severely damaged, but yet one's eyes could still see and feel the beauty of the art work that surrounded them, even through all of the damage the great cathedral had endured. There were broken stained glass windows, small and great statues alike with pieces of clay missing from their faces and limbs. The once beautiful purple velvet material that caressed the great altar hung in tattered thin pieces, dressed just as the people present in the Great Cathedral. But none of that mattered anymore, as riches and fine clothing meant nothing, for to go without hunger and thirst is all that really mattered now. St. John's accepted all those faithful and loyal to God, regardless of what Religion they had been a part of. There were Christians of all faiths, Jews, Moslems, Catholics, and Hindus; all gathered together for one common purpose; to worship their God. Felicia and her family were in the very front row along with Sara, Joe and Byron. All waited patiently for Father Vincent to ascend the altar, and as the Priest stepped upon the altar to begin the long, time-honored ritual of the Holy Mass, Billy was seated between Byron and Joe in his usual state of limbo. To the right of the great altar facing the congregation, stood a large, but odd looking statue that had not been there the week before. As everyone stood to honor Father Vincent for the beginning of the Mass, Billy's eyes flinched with movement, but no-one noticed, and Billy cried out within himself.

"If only I could talk, if only I could move my legs, if only I could show them that I understand their words when they speak to me".

He thought to himself that he must try harder, for he felt trapped in his own body with a brain that refused him freedom of speech or movement. He had to pray harder, he thought to himself. Billy had to make something happen for it was a constant battle cry that only he could hear within himself as he suddenly realized his eyes had moved to gaze upon the half-faced statue on the altar, and a feeling of excitement and hope came over him. He told himself that he would concentrate on this statue, and in his Apache mind, this was an omen of good luck. Billy imagined that the statue had willed his eyes to look upon it, beckoning him to solve the great mystery of what it was, and as he fixed his gaze upon the statue, no-one noticed except he and the statue. From its slightly curved shape, it looked like it could be a woman, and he gazed down at its feet which wore faded brown colored sandals that were similar to those worn by the Romans so many thousands of years ago. He noticed that two toes on one foot were cracked and the toes on the other foot were completely gone. Billy's eyes then slowly wandered up the body of the statue and he thought the clothing also looked similar to what a Roman soldier would have also worn so many of those ancient years before.

"Was this a soldier"?, Billy questioned in his mind.

The statue's hands were empty with each hand held above the other in a half-clenched manner, as if it were at one time grasping an object. His eyes then gently wandered to the one side of it's face that had not been gouged away by years of time and war. The face had a feminine, soft and rosey glow to it with an alabaster finish equal to nothing he had ever seen. At the site of her face, a feeling of inner strength and comfort enveloped him, for she had the face of an angel, he thought; but yet, she was dressed like a man. Perched upon its left shoulder were a pair of bird's talons without the bird's body attached to them, and this also must have broken off of the statue, he thought. By this time, Billy was totally intrigued with the statue, wondering what it could be and as he gazed at the statue, he noticed some type of engraving at its base, but from where he was sitting, he couldn't make the letters out. A feeling of anticipation flowed through him as his eyes quickly searched the statue hoping for a glimpse of wings to confirm his feelings. If only he could get closer to examine her more thoroughly, he thought. Maybe she had wings and he just couldn't see them or maybe they had been broken off. Billy had a strong feeling that she was compelling him to solve her mystery with the promise and faith that God would restore his body back to his control.

Father Vincent faced the people to end the Mass.

"Go in Peace, the Mass is ended"

and everyone stood as Father Vincent spoke these words, and then he told the congregation that the meal would be served as he blessed them. Billy had been so enthralled with the statue that he had hardly noticed the mass was over as Joe and Byron picked him up and placed him in his wheelchair. Both families filed out of the pew and patiently waited in line to descend the steps to the huge basement beneath the Church and enjoy their long-awaited meal. Angella tugged at her Grandmother's blouse, as she placed her hand into Felicia's.

"Grandma, I'm so very happy and excited today, and I love you so very much."

Felicia smiled and hugged her grand-daughter as she gently squeezed Angella's hand.

"I love you too, and Happy Birthday, Angella."

The congregation of at least 200 people were now seated at the long banquet tables, talking to each other while waiting for their meal. Both Sara and Felicia had high hopes of moving into the safety of the Church. Sara and her family were also on the waiting list, but there were no special circumstances that would favor Sara's family moving in for a very long time yet. Father Vincent entered the dining hall to take his seat at the front of the congregation beside his three counterparts. As he passed by Felicia's table, Felicia got his attention and Vincent stooped toward her, as she whispered in his ear. He then pleasantly nodded, and with a grin on his face, resumed his stride to take his place for the meal. No live animals were allowed to be killed for food, as this was strictly forbidden, and rationing of water was also strictly supervised. Humanity had changed its eating habits since the Great War began and because of this crisis situation, mankind could not risk the total extinction of the few domestic animals that had survived. The women of the families who were fortunate enough to live within the confines of the Cathedral, earned their keep by preparing the food, making breads and pastas, and serving the hungry families of the congregation. There was also a great store room filled with canned and dry goods left over from the war that could support them for at least another 2 full years or more, thanks to Rabbi Silverman who brought what food-stuffs he had salvaged from his devastated Temple. With the help of Pastor Bennett, Father Vincent had also worked tirelessly to start a farm on several acres adjacent to the Cathedral. Through their efforts, they now had many chickens to lay eggs and they also had a small herd of dairy cows that supplied milk for the babies and young children. Father Thomas, the Greek priest, and his parishioners contributed by bringing all of their bottled water to add to the Cathedral's supply. There was still so much to be done and they were finally starting to make some progress, but Father Vincent prayed to God that nature would somehow return, so there could be more hope in cultivation; for he hoped to keep the people from total starvation until the process of complete rejuvenation could somehow be fulfilled. However, nature and man were running out of time, and this worried Father Vincent. Angella's eyes widened in disbelief as large terrines of vegetable soup were placed on each table along with baskets of freshly baked bread, followed by trays of potatoes, carrots, beans, and pasta. Father Vincent bowed his head and said a prayer thanking God for this wonderful gift of food to help humanity survive. The whole congregation then began to enjoy their meal and as they savored every morsel, they talked, laughed, and enjoyed each other's company. Felicia and Sara took turns helping to feed Billy, for even though he could somewhat move his arms, he still had difficulty feeding himself. Just as the meal was being finished, Father Vincent stood in front of the congregation to speak.

"Everyone, May I have your attention". "I have a special announcement to make".

"We have a Happy Birthday celebration for one of our children who is 7 years old today".

Father Vincent looked straight at Angella and smiled, asking

Angella to Please Stand Up, for it was her very own special day. Angella blushed as everyone clapped loudly, and Father Vincent then continued.

"To celebrate Angella's birthday, we have a special treat". "However, we only have about 100 of these to go around; so many of you will have to share with your neighbor and I hope none of you will mind that".

Father Vincent nodded to one of the women workers, and to Angella's surprise, four huge trays of chocolate frosted cupcakes were brought out to the tables. The congregation stood and began singing 'Happy Birthday' to Angella, and as they sang, a large frosted cupcake with one white, little candle, was placed before Angella, as she stood gazing at her first "birthday cake". Her eyes watered and a tear of happiness ran down her cheek as she made a wish before blowing out the candle. This was the best birthday she ever had and she would remember this day for the rest of her life. Felicia watched as Angella blew out the little white candle, and Felicia was happy knowing that she and Father Vincent had given her grand-daughter a truly wonderful gift this day; the gift of a beautiful memory that Angella would cherish forever. Felicia and Sara waited patiently to speak with Father Vincent. Byron and Joe sat quietly with Billy at the end of the long dining table, while Sam went to check on Chief. Father Vincent said his goodbyes to the few remaining people that were filtering out of the banquet hall, and when they were gone, he then turned and approached Felicia, and she could see that he looked very tired. He was a man of about 50, of average height, quite slender, and usually dressed in his work clothes, for he very rarely wore his priest's collar or robes, as they too were also becoming tattered, and so to save them, he would only wear them when he said Mass or on very special occasions. Father Vincent was the type of man that never complained and worked obsessively to try to make things better, but Felicia could see the frustration and worry in his face.

"Father Vincent, Are you feeling alright"?

"Does it show that much", he said in his soft-spoken manner.

"Felicia, I have so very much to do and there just doesn't seem to be enough time to accomplish all that I know I must".

Felicia smiled as Father Vincent asked her what he could do for her?

"Please, Father Vincent; Can you make room for my family?".

He looked at her with sad eyes.

"Felicia, there is no more room within the Cathedral right now and the parish house is full, and I really don't know what to say or do anymore; for there are so many needy people who need refuge".

Felicia had to think fast to come up with some sort of idea to change Father Vincent's mind.

"Father Vincent", she blurted out, "it's getting more difficult for us to take care of Billy". "We could stay down here in the basement and I can help teach the children their school lessons and"...

but before she could finish her sentence, Sam entered the room with Chief, and interrupted by saying.

"and I can help you with the animals and the farm work, and Chief will be our guard dog".

"He'll protect you too, Father Vincent"., added Sam.

Before Vincent could get a word in, Joe and Sara joined in the conversation, as Joe spoke up and told Father Vincent that he and Byron could help with new construction and maintenance work in the repair and rebuilding of anything Father Vincent needed to be done. Sara then added her voice to the others by saying she would help with the food preparation, cleaning, and nursing. Father Vincent plopped down in his chair and rubbed his forehead in frustration as both families stood motionless and no other words were said, for they hoped and prayed he would let them stay. Out of the stillness and quiet of that moment, one small voice was heard as Angella tapped Father Vincent on his knee.

"Father Vincent, thank you for the first birthday party and the very first birthday cake I ever had".

"I'll always love and remember you."

Father Vincent looked up to see the love, truth, and innocence in Angella's face and eyes. He wrapped his arms around her and hugged her.

"How can I refuse an angel of a child"?

"Yes, Yes, he stated; you can all stay".

"Somehow, we'll find room for all of you".

They were overtaken with tears of joy and they bent in thanks before him.

"Please, "Please. don't kneel before me". "Kneel before God only".

"Thank him and thank Angella".

There were three separate sections of the huge underground basement that sat beneath the Cathedral. One section contained the underground kitchen and banquet room, and another huge section contained the inventory area where the food and water were stored. Adjacent to that, were three concrete steps that led down to an older part of the original foundation. Father Vincent had almost forgotten it existed until one of the workers wandered into the area and found a very old statue that had once graced the Cathedral many hundreds of years ago. Billy's eyes widened in surprise at the sound of these words, and no-one noticed except Chief. Father Vincent explained that this part of the basement had been used as a wine and fruit cellar more than 200 or 300 years ago. He then got a flashlight to lead the way, for it was really quite dark in that area, but it would be a very cool and welcome place to rest, out of reach from the intense rays of the sun. Both families jubilantly followed Father Vincent down the steps and into their new home. The area was at least 700 square feet separated by a short half-wall, and at the end of the room was a very small, curved 5 feet high open archway. Father Vincent explained that he thought it led to the other chamber that was used as a fruit cellar at one time, but had never taken the time to really investigate it. The priest also told them he had much to show and explain to them, but he must get some rest, and invited them to join the workers in the banquet hall for an early breakfast of bread and coffee. After breakfast, he would then discuss all they needed to know, so both families thanked Father Vincent and asked for his blessing. Felicia, Angella, and Sara were excitedly making plans for their new home while Joe, along with Byron and Sam, went to gather their meager belongings at the parking lot. Chief sat beside Billy ever watchful and instinctively sniffed the air with his large sensitive nostrils. The two families finished getting their new home in order while Billy wished he could help, as Joe supervised the boys by telling them where to put the sleeping mats. Felicia and Sara were deciding where to place each candle, to afford them an even flow of light throughout the wine cellar while Angella happily followed them around at the placement of each beautiful candle, which she would then light. When at last the final candle was lit, everyone gathered together and basked in the warm and gentle glow cast upon the room. After Joe and Byron placed Billy on his mat, Felicia hugged everyone goodnight as by this time, they were all visibly tired and ready to retire. She went to her section of the room where she plopped down onto her sleeping mat, for it had been a very long and exciting day.

"Grandma, you don't have to tell us that story tonight", said Angella.

"I'm so tired that I'd probably fall asleep and never hear the end of it anyway".

"Do you mind, Grandma"?

Felicia chuckled softly.

"No, dear", she said. "I don't mind at all".

Angella continued....

"Grandma, today was a dream come true for me, and you were right", "It was the best birthday I ever dreamed of having and my birthday wish came true".

"You must have made two wishes because my dream came true too", added Sam.

"I can't believe I'm really going to help Father Vincent on the farm with the animals".

"All of our wishes came true", stated Felicia, as her eyes dreamily danced with happiness.

Sam and Angella said good night and went to their beds with Chief, and Felicia thought to herself how good it was to finally be in a dark and cool room away from the sun's hot rays. The flickering glow from the candles reminded her of how the moon used to cast its soft and muted reflections on the earth, never to be felt or seen again; and Oh, how she missed the moon and its different faces. In her mind, Felicia relived the day's events and thanked God that he had smiled on them as she closed her eyes and quickly fell asleep.

CHAPTER 2

It was peaceful and quiet in the candle lit wine cellar but Chief's eyes were not completely shut even though he appeared to be sleeping. Now and then his right ear would perk up when he heard the sound of snoring as he steadfastly remained between the children. Within the peace and quiet of the moment, a soft-spoken, but yet compelling voice called to him.

"Apollo", "Apollo of Dogs, come to me."

His eyes opened widely and his large proud head snapped to immediate attention as he flexed his sensitive ears upward to their maximum height and listened intently. Again, the voice called to him

"Apollo of Dogs, Creature of the Lord, come to me if you are to protect your master and humanity."

Unable to move or cry out, Billy also heard the voice and at first he thought he was dreaming until he saw Chief get up and move through the curved opening that led through the fruit cellar. Billy watched anxiously as Chief disappeared around the corner and to his amazement, something very mysteriously happened. As Chief disappeared from view, Billy's mind became his eyes and they followed the dog, as Chief took loping strides down a corridor and into another passageway that led to an underground cavern.

"How could this be"?, Billy thought;

and it was as if Billy was there every step of the way with Chief. Billy didn't understand what was happening but there was nothing he could do about it, and suddenly he was terrified. Each stride was taken with commanding power and grace as Chief moved toward the shimmering soft rays of light in the distance. He seemed to know exactly where he was going and when he drew near to the light, he stopped and stretched his head forward and gingerly sniffed the air. Billy's mind was there with him, seeing the beautiful soft rainbow colors of light slowly floating through the air in all directions, but no-one could be seen as the voice again was heard. It was a soothing voice filled with compassion and power, for as it spoke, it matched the warmth and radiance of the shimmering rays of light.

"Apollo of Dogs",

"Ancestors who have been faithful to mankind since the beginning of time; your Creator calls you."

Chief whimpered as if he understood what the voice was saying and moved closer to the glowing crystal-colored particles of light. The soothing voice continued

"All created by the Lord must and shall survive, great loyal friend".

"Lead the three young man-races to me along with the priest and first-mother within 3 full days of the sun star."

"Go now, Chief, and watch over them."

Chief tilted his head and uttered a soft bark before he slowly retreated from the light to return to the wine cellar, and as he rounded the last corner, he walked through the curved open doorway that led into the room. He momentarily stood in the middle of the room to survey his surroundings as if he were making sure that no-one was missing. As he turned to take his place between Sam and Angella, he suddenly lowered his head and stared directly into Billy's eyes, and as their eyes met, Chief instinctively knew that Billy was also favored by the voice of the light. Even though he no longer felt afraid, Billy was still in shock at what he had just experienced;

"What was this heavenly voice?

"What did this voice look like"?

He wondered why he was being allowed to see and hear this great vision through his mind, but yet without physically being a part of it; and then he turned his thoughts to the statue in the Cathedral.

"Was it her voice, he thought"?

In his heart he truly believed the statue was somehow connected to this supernatural experience. Already, two full days had quickly passed and Father Vincent put Joe in charge of building a new addition to the existing parish house so he could grant more people refuge. Joe and his son Byron worked together along with 30 other men to accomplish this task and Joe was happy working side by side with his son, for Byron seemed to be more grownup in those 2 days as he had learned quickly from his father on how to do things. Some of the men would ask Byron questions before asking his father, and this made Joe feel proud knowing that the other men respected Byron. Every morning after mass, Father Vincent and Sam went to the farm to take care of the animals and collect the eggs from the hen house. Father Vincent was amazed at how the animals were drawn to Sam and there was not one animal on the farm who feared him, for they seemed to gravitate toward Sam as if he were a magnet, and Millie a dairy cow, followed him everywhere like a puppy dog. Felicia's schedule was also very busy because school started right after breakfast and Father Vincent gave her the early morning class of 20 children whom she was to teach the basic three R's, and then adding any other subjects she wished to teach. Angella was also in the class which made things nice for both of them, and afterward, Felicia joined Sara in the kitchen to help prepare and serve the meals, while Angella and the other children set the long dining tables and also helped with the cleanup chores. It was a full day's work for all of them but they loved every minute of it, and even Chief's days were full of fun and excitement as he tried to keep up with everyone. First, he would run to the construction site at the Parish House and watch Byron and the others work. After surveying and sniffing over the situation, he would then run at top speed to the farm where he had the most fun, for Sam would let him through the gate and they would have a game of catch ball. After a short playtime, Sam would then clean up the barn and hen house, always under Chief's watchful eye. When the work was done, they headed back to the Cathedral and Chief's first stop was, naturally, the kitchen where his food and water were always waiting for him. At the end of each day's work, both families relaxed in their cozy little wine cellar, discussing what they had accomplished. Byron lived up to his promise and began teaching Sam how to box, and on many evenings, Sara would sing and encouraged everyone to join her as they shared their happiness and new home together. They were having such great fun enjoying their new life that they didn't want to remember the rest of the world's suffering, for they felt safe and secure in their wonderful new surroundings. They were all fast asleep except Billy, for he began to feel anxious as he anticipated the moment when he would surely hear that voice again. He was very restless as he glanced at Chief for a sign of some kind, but when nothing happened, he tried to get some rest. Chief looked as calm as could be, just lying in his usual spot guarding Sam and Angella as always, so Billy closed his eyes for a brief moment to envision the statue, when suddenly the soft-spoken voice echoed in his mind.

"Chief, beloved creature, bring them to me."

"I will help you gather them."

Billy's eyes excitedly opened to see Chief quietly and calmly get up as he gingerly tugged on Sam's arm to wake him. When Sam finally woke up, he was surprised to see that Chief was standing over him and Sam was about to say something, but as he looked at Chief's face in the candle lit room, everything was made clear. Sam nodded his head in agreement as if he had read Chief's mind, but somehow he felt as if he were still dreaming. After Sam woke the others from their sleep, Chief quietly led them through the opening of the archway to the fruit cellar, where they sat down on the ground. The gentle voice was then heard filtering within their minds

"Do not be afraid, for no harm will come to you."

"You will wait here until Chief returns with the Priest and then he will show you the way".

Even though the voice was calm and soothing, Felicia felt somewhat uneasy as she tried to conceal her true feelings from the children. Byron was still a little sleepy as he asked,

"What's going on, Man"?

Sam replied; "I don't know Byr, Byron, but I guess we'll soon find out".

"Grandma, don't be afraid",

"You know Chief wouldn't do anything to hurt us", Angella emphatically stated.

Felicia hoped that Father Vincent would know what to do as she hovered close to the children and waited impatiently wondering what was going on. Billy also wondered why Sara and Joe were not awakened, for they were in a very deep sleep and then he thought that maybe the voice didn't want them to know anything yet, for there must be a reason and some kind of a plan. He felt very sure of that as he wished and hoped that he could really be a part of it physically, and then he thought that he must try harder to move his legs, but as hard as he tried, they wouldn't move. Father Vincent was alone in the Church, kneeling at the first step before God's altar in prayer when Chief entered the Great Cathedral and his claws could be heard scraping the marble floor beneath him as he moved down the center aisle toward the altar. Father Vincent was startled by the sound and so as he quickly turned to look over his shoulder, he felt relieved but yet surprised when he saw that it was Chief.

"My goodness, "What are you doing in here"?

Chief began whimpering and pawing at the priest's garments.

"What is it Boy? What do you want"?

Chief then barked and began tugging on the priest's arm, entreating Vincent to come with him.

"Okay, something must be wrong, so lead the way".

Chief led Vincent to the others in the fruit cellar and upon seeing them huddled together, he was bewildered. "What are you doing in here"?

Felicia was about to tell him what happened, when the voice

was heard.

"Do not fear, for you should feel honored to have been chosen above all others."

"Apollo of dogs, lead them to me".

They all looked at each other in amazement at the sound of the voice and in it's words, for even though they were mystified and speechless, the voice was like music to their ears.

"Come, we will follow Chief", Vincent stated.

Chief was exhuberant as he smoothly pranced with pride and great strength down the pathway that led into the hidden cavern, and the small group of humanity that followed him were in awe of all they saw and so was Billy, for his mind and eyes were there with them. When Chief turned the last corner, the dazzling crystals of light shown brighter and brighter sending out sparks of every color known to man as their rays sent dancing arcs of celestial light illuminating the wondrous cave. From the floor of the cavern, cone-shaped and milky stalagmites grew incredibly upward, nearly touching the awesome stalactite formations which hung like giant clusters of frosty icicles from the cavern's ceiling above.

As the group ventured deeper within the cavern, the Holy Light could be clearly seen as it drew them closer until Chief stopped and sat directly before it, and from the direction of the light, the serene, but yet magnetizing voice was heard.

"You have done well, loyal creature of the Almighty One."

Upon hearing these words, Chief then moved to the left side of the light and patiently waited while the small group of humanity stood frozen in time. The voice continued speaking as multi-colored diamond crystal particles forged through layers of several large limestone rocks, revealing a figure that emerged. As the celestial being moved toward them, the almost blinding crystal particles became softly subdued for they now flowed inward and around the entity that was approaching.

"Do not be afraid, children, for no harm will come to you", as the voice spoke to them from the rainbow flames of soft hues.

The vision was now in full view as it stopped 10 feet before them with glowing crystal particles radiating from within and around it's body. She was a towering figure of at least 7 to 8 feet tall, an ultimate creation of unspeakable beauty and magnificent power, but as she moved a little closer to them, the height of her body reduced to that of being more human. Her skin was the color of a spectacular, yet soft golden amber topaz with a crowning glory of hair that was slightly below shoulder length, and made up of a series of incredible golden sun-lit hues with a heavenly bronze brilliance streaked throughout. Three pulsating headbands of gold caressed her forehead and temples as her silken and bronze-streaked hair gently flowed beneath them. Her eyebrows were femininely arched to match the bone structure of her exquisite amber face and were a soft shade of Lilac, as were her lips to match her brilliant, soul-searching, Amethyst eyes and long eyelashes, also of God's most passionate violet color. Her cheeks had the soft blush of a warm Bronze and the radiance of love in her face calmed them. Her feet were simply dressed in light bronze sandals with straps that stopped just above her ankles and in her right hand, she held a filigree-carved, wooden staff. Covering the length of her right forearm, she wore a golden mesh-like band fringed with strands of pure platinum and studded with rubies, sapphires, garnets, emeralds, topaz, amethyst, diamonds, aquamarine, and alexandrite; all intermingled with brilliant crushed crystals. Another golden band graced her left forearm which was covered in Jade, moonstone, turquoise, obsidian, lapis luzi, agates, pearls, jasper, rhodonite, opals, rose quartz, and malachite; and these were interspersed with glowing crystals and ice blue zircons. All of the gems and ores of the world graced her great beauty, but yet she wore the clothing of a Roman Soldier entering into battle. They were enthralled and mesmerized at the breathtaking image before them as they stood silent and questioned their minds daring not to ask, but Billy already knew who she was. This being of splendidness could read their minds and answered.

"I am Allestra-Terra, Archangel of the 9th Power who dwells

in the 5th House of Dominus, and Protector of His Holy Waters of Creation."

Overwhelmed with emotion, they looked at each other with wonder in their eyes.

"Grandma, you said angels had wings", Angella blurted out.

Allestra smiled as she spoke directly to Angella,

"Little angel of earth, you have brought a smile to my lips and to God's Heart".

With that, Father Vincent drew on his courage to speak.

"Why did you seek us out"?

Allestra moved her staff forward

"Behold God's Light and Truth."

As she tilted her staff, a pulsating, glowing white light could be seen within the filigree-carved figures of her staff, lighting each figure as it made it's way upward. As the illuminating light slowly approached the top of her staff, a magnificent, Diamond Pyramid Crystal emerged in glory to rest at the very top of the staff, sending out dazzling rays of the colors of infinity in all directions of the cavern, enrapturing them in the illumination and warmth of Dominus. Allestra-Terra then pointed the giant Crystal toward the ground as it then glowed into a brilliant rich Amethyst, and a glorious spring of heavenly deep purple and blue water bubbled up from beneath the ground. As the whirlpool of energized waters swirled before them, Allestra then raised her staff and the crystal returned to its natural diamond radiance. Allestra-Terra looked toward the priest and then to the whole group.

"I will give you the answers to all of your questions but you must listen well to my words."

"In the beginning, The Lord, Dominus, created the World, all of nature and its elements including the Holy Waters which became the seas and rivers of the earth."

"He created the creatures and placed them on the earth and He created Mankind to enjoy this beautiful Paradise, for his love is boundless toward his most precious creation of Man".

"Because the Creator is Perfect, he knew the day would come

when the waters of the earth and all that He so lovingly created would become contaminated to suffer a slow death, and so he separated a small portion of the Holy Waters and called upon the 5th House of Archangels to come to Him."

"The Lord, Dominus, then highly honored me for I was chosen to protect the Waters of Creation until they would be needed."

Sam and Byron excitedly interrupted Allestra.

"You mean you're going to give us the Water"? Byron asked.

Sam then added, "Can we have some now"?

Allestra replied........"It is not as easy as that, for no human can touch these waters, for they are as they were first created and touched only by the Hand of God, and are therefore still holy and pure."

"If any human or creature touches the water in it's present state, They Will Die, for besides God, Only an Archangel can touch them."

"Dear Angel of God, Why do you protect the Water, and from whom"? asked Felicia.

Allestra-Terra paused as she stared at Father Vincent and asked him,

"Priest of God, dost thou know the answer?"

With a lump in his throat, Father Vincent looked at Allestra, and hesitated before answering.

"Yes, pure Angel".

Again the priest hesitated.

"It frightens me to even think that it could be"....

Allestra prodded him by saying,

"Please speak Vincent, Do not be afraid".

Vincent spoke the only words he could,

"It is the light that once was".

"It is Lucifer".

"You protect the waters from he who now calls himself Satan."

The children and Felicia were startled by what Father Vincent had just said and Allestra did not smile, for she knew she must go on to tell them what they needed to know.

"Because of Lucifer's hatred toward God, the world and mankind has suffered through many wars, persecution, and injustice."

"He has tempted man and has gained many souls since the beginning of time to hurt the Lord".

"The world is on the brink of total death and darkness, and if Satan gains control of the Holy Waters, he will use them to blackmail what is left of humanity into giving up their very souls to him, for he knows they are desperately clinging to this life."

"This would bring great sorrow and pain to God who loves Humanity, for if the unholy one accomplishes this deed, he then brings his Hell to earth to rule over humanity, and they will suffer many cruel torments at his hand; more evil and cruel than any war imaginable, as mankind will live for eternity shackled to Satan's Hell."

"And, this is how Satan proposes to stab God's Heart and all that he has created and loved, as Satan has already contaminated the earth with his vile touch, for he despises God and Mankind."

"So therefore, I protect the Waters, for Satan lurks nearby and will come here soon to do battle for them."

"Why were we chosen"?, asked Byron.

Sam then questioned, "How can we help a Mighty Archangel"?

Allestra moved a little closer to them for she knew that she had put fear into their hearts and souls. In her compassionate and beautiful voice, she continued:

"I not only protect the waters, but I represent all of the colors of Humanity."

As she spoke, she moved directly in front of Byron and her pyramid crystal glowed into a magnificent blue Sapphire, and an exact duplicate of herself formed out of her body, as Allestra-Terra of the black-race appeared before them. They were in profound awe as Allestra of the black race stood before them with her forehead adorned in three headbands; one band comprised of the Topaz gem in its royal colors of amber, rose, blue and green. Her middle band was that of pure gold, followed by a third band of Red Coral. She was dressed as the first ancient Nubian representing the lands of Africa and mother unto the birth of Egypt. On her finger, she wore a Lapis Lazuli carved in the likeness of a dome and set in gold, for this was the ring adopted by Egypt's mighty Pharoahs; thus acknowledging Byron's powerful ancestors many thousands of years before him. Allestra-Terra then moved toward Sam as the Crystal turned into a glorious, vibrant Emerald, and an exact duplicate of herself formed out of her body as Allestra of the Red-race emerged and stood before them. Again, the group was struck with the splendor before them as her elegant high cheek bones and facial features were highlighted by her beautiful headbands of Indian blue Turquoise, one of pure gold, and a solid band of the Healing Bloodstone. At the bottom of each of her long black braids, hung the magnificent feathers of the blood brothers; one of the golden eagle and the other of the bald eagle. Perched upon her shoulder was the Great Golden Eagle who had guided the peoples of the indomitable Red Race over the vast ice tundras into the land of Sam's ancestors and of all the Indian tribes, many thousands of years before. Allestra then progressed to the priest, Angella, and Felicia, as the Crystal radiated into the brilliance of the Lord of gems; the Royal Star Ruby, and Allestra of the Caucasian-race formed out of her body taking her place before the group. Her flowing auburn/chestnut hair glistened with profound radiance as it's mane-like thickness was adorned with headbands of ancient Imperial Jasper, one of pure gold, and one of dazzling crystals, signifying all of the cultures of the white race embracing Europe, the Middle East, India, and beyond to the secret race who did not sin. In her hands she held the crossed staffs of Eden and Atlantis, safeguarding the powers and secrets of infinity. Allestra-Terra then returned in front of the small group as the angels of colors gently filtered back into her body and the Crystal returned to its original diamond luster and radiance. Allestra-Terra continued to explain that,

"God has given me unequaled power to defeat Satan, for I represent all of the Human races that He has created, but there is one missing; and in order for me to be truly powerful and complete, I must have one of the yellow race present here to stand with you against Satan."

"I cannot leave this place to seek one of the Yellow Race, for if I leave, Satan will seize the opportunity to steal the Waters of Creation."

"Through centuries of my protection, a few of purity have come into the cavern but the time was not yet right.

"God has chosen you because you are truly good in heart and spirit, for the eon has now come." "I will guide and protect you always on your journey".

With her divine eyes, she stared at Sam and Byron.

"Brothers, you will go on a journey to find at least one of the Yellow Race and the Apollo of Dogs will guide you, for evil will come to you and show it's face"..

Felicia began to worry as she heard Allestra's words. How could she send two young boys out into the hostile land knowing they would encounter evil. Allestra answered Felicia knowing she was uneasy. "Felicia, have faith, for they will be protected."

"Satan will come here three times to tempt me into giving him the Water."

"You must return with one of the Yellow Race within three days, for Satan comes on the third visit prepared to battle and I must be complete".

Turning to Father Vincent and Felicia,

"Both of you will help gather mankind to the Cathedral."

"How are we to do this"?, asked Father Vincent?

Allestra then took off one of the golden bands from her forehead and it pulsated with luminous sparks of fluid gold within her hands, as she bowed her head in reverence.

In her innocent little voice,

"It's your halo isn't it", said Angella excitedly.

Allestra grinned broadly at the little girl as the rest of the group chuckled, but were surprised at Allestra's answer.

"Yes, Precious One",

"This is the "Nimbus", "symbolic of grace and virtue, for it is also called "THE CIRCLE OF ETERNAL LIFE."

Allestra-Terra raised the golden Nimbus over her head as it continued sending out radiant sparks of glorious fluid Gold, growing larger and larger as it slowly loomed upward until it was completely out of their site.

"The Circle of Eternal Life has been cast 7 earth miles around this House of God."

"All may enter the Circle and those within it who love and believe in God will be saved, and because of their strong faith, ALL of humanity that is good will be saved; but all Evil shall be cast out".

"Father Vincent and Felicia will prepare to warn as many as they can for the coming battle they will witness."

Allestra moved very close to Angella and bent down beside her as she spoke.

"Little angel of God, you have reached the age of 7, the age of reason and perfection, for You are most pure in soul and innocent of heart."

"God wishes you to learn much, so I will help teach you, for you will guide others in the future about what has happened here, and you will keep these words for your children and all generations that shall follow." "There is much for you to learn and You will come and visit me tomorrow so we can begin."

A heavenly glow shown in Angella's face as Allestra moved away from the group and slowly returned to the back of the cavern until they could no longer see her.

"Remember what I have told you this day." "God loves you and will protect you."

Chief joined Sam as the five of them walked back through the cavern, still in shock and amazement at what they had witnessed, and none of them could get Allestra's image out of their minds and hearts. Before they reached their rooms, Father Vincent had already began to make plans and he decided that after Mass, he would prepare Byron and Sam for their journey with plenty of food and water for they must obey Allestra and leave as soon as possible. Felicia and he would then have a meeting on how to warn and prepare as many people as they could for what was about to occur.

The next day had begun very quickly for all of them, and as was the custom, all of the people that lived at the Cathedral gathered together to start their day with prayer. After prayers, Father Vincent told them of the Great Impending Battle between Satan and the Archangel, but from their facial expressions, Father Vincent was saddened because he could tell that many of them did not believe. Billy kept his eyes on the statue as he faithful prayed for the return of his voice so that he may speak again, and as he looked at the statue, he noticed it looked as if it had somewhat been repaired. One of the feet that had no toes, was suddenly complete with all of its toes.

"How could this be"?

"This could not be the work of man".

Billy knew it must be the work of Allestra and as he looked upon the statue, he pictured Allestra in his mind and he again freventy prayed to regain his speech. After Mass, Father Vincent was visibly upset, for already half of the congregation had gone and only the true Believers were left. As both families approached Father Vincent, Sara and Joe knelt before the altar and told Father Vincent

"We love the Lord and will do all that we can to help, and we thank Him, knowing our son was one that was chosen, they said."

Father Vincent had prepared food, water, and clean clothing for Sam and Byron.

"I have even given you some extra food and water for Chief", smiled Vincent as he gave them a special blessing of protection for their journey. Sara and Joe hugged Byron and said their goodbyes while Felicia and Angella held Sam close, not wanting to let go. As the two boys prepared to leave the Cathedral, a voice yelled out.

"No". "No" "Wait." .

Everyone turned and looked in amazement to see that it was Billy who had spoken. "S a m. S a m". Billy strained to formulate his son's name out of his mouth as Sam ran to his father along with Felicia and the others.

"Dad, Dad". "Oh, My God, Dad". "You talked."

Billy was excited and impatient to get more words out and as he spoke, his arms moved much easier to embrace Sam.

"Sam, I love you". "You have been a good son to me and, God, the Great Spirit will be with you, and Chief will guide you".

As they hugged each other, Sam looked into his father's eyes for no other words were necessary and then the families and Father Vincent watched in silence as Byron, Sam, and Chief left the Great Cathedral. Even though Billy had regained his speech, he was still paralyzed from the waist down, but he thanked God for the return of his speech, and he was overcome as tears welled up in his eyes. He told Felicia and the rest of them how the voice of the angel had called to Chief and how he had seen and heard everything at the Cavern when Allestra beckoned them. As they looked at Billy and heard him speak, they knew this was a great miracle and they hoped that someday Billy would walk. They went to the great banquet hall to meet with the other priests of God to prepare their plans, as Allestra had told them to do, and they came up with a plan to offer a meal, without the designated food tickets, so as to draw more people into the Circle of Eternal Life and into the Church. They hoped in their hearts that the people who would come would have true faith in God so that mankind could be saved at the time of the Great Battle, as Allestra had told them.

"Grandma, I think I should go to visit Allestra now." "Would you walk me part of the way"?

Felicia put her arms around her grand-daughter and guided her through the fruit cellar and into the cavern.

Once Felicia saw the light sparkle at the back of the cavern, she stopped.

"You're not afraid Angella, are you"?

"No, Grandma, not anymore".

"I know she's there now because I see the light".

"I'll watch you from here until you get to the light and then

I'll come back later when you're ready to come home", said Felicia.

"Yes Grandma", Angella replied,

and so Felicia watched her grand-daughter until she could faintly see her go into the light. Allestra walked toward Angella and sat down on a large multi-colored boulder. She was very plainly dressed in a white flowing gown which was tied at the waist with ribbons of crushed moonstones. Her skin tone was a soft warm bronze color, glowing and highlighted by her wondrous amethyst brows and large, loving eyes of the same royal color. Her neck was wrapped in a heavenly white fabric laden with pink crystals and studded with magnificent marquis cut Amethysts forming an elongated stellar-cross that matched her eyebrows and eyes.

"Little Angel, you may come and sit by me if you wish".

"I love you for you are an innocent child of God.", said Allestra.

Angella sat beside the Archangel and looked at her skin.

Angella asked, "May I touch you"?

With a girlish laugh on her lips, Allestra nodded her head in delight;

"Yes, Angella; you may touch me as I am now".

Angella touched the angel's face and was surprised to find that it felt as warm and alive as her own. Angella looked at Allestra's body as if she were searching for something, and then asked

"Where are your wings"?

Allestra broadly smiled and answered the little girl's question.

"Archangels are Warriors and different from God's other angels, and besides, sometimes wings get in the way". "Do you need to see wings to prove that I have or have not"?

Angella had a puzzled look on her face as she tried to understand what Allestra was saying.

"Angella, if I believe you are an angel, do I need to really see your wings to prove it"?

"Oh! said Angella, "I understand now".

"I must have faith".

"Just because I don't see them with my eyes, doesn't mean you don't have them or that you're not an Angel".

"Good, Good". "That is what Faith means", replied Allestra.

"As you grow older little one, you will be beloved by all, for you will be a great teacher in the new world to come".

"God has chosen you to teach mankind that all colors of race must listen to their hearts and honor and respect one another; for they must remember that although they may be of different colors; each of their souls is but one color, for they are Mankind".

Angella nodded her head in agreement as Allestra's radiance illuminated Angella's face and sweet, innocent eyes.

"It is almost time for you to go now, but I will watch over you as you return to your grandmother".

Allestra watched Angella until she saw Felicia greet the little girl and knew that they were safe, for the Archangel's face soon turned to an expression of great caution as her eyes darted from side to side and her nostrils flared open. Allestra could feel and smell the evil coming closer as she quietly sat upon the boulder as a heavy, thumping sound of walking in the distance could be heard. (His feet were bare and hideously deformed with long thick gray arched-down toes and nails. A small charcoal fragment of a once-honorable wing that signified his rank, protruded just above each ankle bone; but as he moved deeper into the cavern, his feet were now bound in a pair of black shoes, so as not to reveal himself.). The tall handsome young man of about 35 with jet black hair and deep green eyes stumbled into the cavern as if he were lost and trying to find the way back to the Cathedral. He called for help as he walked through the cavern.

"Is anybody here? "Help",

he continued as if in distress, and as he moved forward around the last bend, he saw Allestra sitting on the boulder and subtly approached her.

Allestra lifted her head as she spoke.

"Who goes there"?.

He stopped in his tracks with a look of awe and disbelief upon his face and asked.

"Who are you?"

Softly, the Archangel answered.

"I am Allestra", she said.

"What's a beautiful woman like you doing here"?

"Are you lost too"?.

"Come, we'll find the way out together and who knows, it might be fun and you might want to kiss me as I want to kiss you right now."

Allestra commandingly stood up.

"Satan knows who I am." "Be Gone from this Holy Place."

Confused by what she had said, the young man replied.

"What are you talking about"?

"I don't understand what you're saying".

Allestra drew her wrist bands together and repeated.

"I shall remind thee again of who I am."

"I am Allestra-Terra, 9th Power in the 5th House of the Lord, Protector of the Holy Waters of Creation". "Does Satan now remember?.."

The handsome young man's voice changed to a deep, cruel, inhuman pitch and his beautiful green eyes became black and encircled with slight flickers of deep violet rays. In a sarcastic and sinister tone, he answered Allestra.

"Yes, I know thee Bitch of Light."

"You who are filth and betrayer of thy kind."

"Where is thy Water?"

Allestra clapped her wrist bands together and Crystal colored formations appeared surrounding her with singing angelic voices. Satan was blinded by the site of the Crystals and as he quickly looked away, he also covered his ears for he could not stand the sight nor the sound of heaven, as they were singing praises to the Almighty One.

She powerfully answered him.

"Be gone Father of Evil, for I will destroy thee now".

He defiantly raised his arm forward and answered her in a hideously cruel tone, as he began to leave.

"It is the beginning of the end for thee and I will be back Allestra, for we will talk again and we shall see how really loyal thou art when I take thy soul."

CHAPTER 3

By this time, Sam and Byron had checked out almost every place they could think of searching to find at least one person of the Yellow Race. They had even gone by the parking lot where they used to live and talked to the old man, Carl, who knew of none living there. With Chief leading the way, they were soon out of the City and into an acrid area of land which they had never seen before. They decided to stop and rest near some Manzenita bushes before traveling on and Byron opened his sack, as they shared a little food and water between themselves and Chief.

"I don't know who we're going to find out here, let alone an oriental person", said Byron.

"Allestra said Chief would lead the way", Sam answered.

"I just hope Chief knows where he's going", replied Byron, as he added

"Look we have to stick together at all times, and I brought along my knife just in case we run into trouble, but I just hope I don't have to use it."

Sam looked at the shrubs, and rocks, and the ground beneath his feet and said,

"You know, Byron, this is what it must have been like for my Apache Ancestors when they went out into the Wilderness and came back as Warriors".

"Yeah, Well Okay little Warrior, we better get moving, cause we don't have much time to waste", stated Byron.

The three of them continued on their journey and finally reached the outer edges of the Circle of Eternal Life. Sam and Byron knew it had to be the Circle of Eternal Life for it was a spectacular wonder to behold as billowing vertical sheaths of colors streamed from the earth up toward the heavens as high as the human eye could see. They entered the beautiful mist of different shades of greens, purples, and pinks that were interspersed with twinkling silver and gold flecks, which danced upon their bodies as they cast their glow of what the magnificent earth once reflected from the heavens above. As they passed through the Circle of Eternal Life, they suddenly became afraid and wondered if they should turn back toward the city, for now they felt unprotected. But, they knew they had a mission to accomplish so they traveled onward hoping Chief would find the Yellow One soon. They were now a few miles beyond the Circle of Eternal Life when Chief suddenly stopped and cautiously sniffed the air. To their right was a small mountain of differently shaped rocks and large ledges. Chief quickly began moving toward the ledges while the two boys did the best they could to follow him, and as the dog closed in on the scent, he started barking. There, under one of the huge ledges, was a young oriental girl who was pregnant and half-dead. The boys gently pulled her out from beneath the ledge and splashed some water on her face, hoping she was still alive. As she gained consciousness, she became startled when she first saw them, but then gladly accepted their food and water without hesitation. After she had eaten and drank, Sam asked her what her name was? Timidly, she answered.

"My name is Lynn".

Byron told her not to be afraid of them for they were not there to hurt her or anyone. Sam then asked her what she was doing out in this wasteland all alone. Lynn told them that she and her husband had to leave the city because they feared for their lives and that everyone hated them for what the Yellow Race had done to the world, and how they were shunned and attacked because of this. Lynn also told them that her husband had gone to the City one day to try and get food for them, but he never came back. As time passed, she became terrified at the thought that something awful must have happened to him because he never would have abandoned her and the baby she carried within. Sam told her the story of Allestra and why they were sent to find one of the Yellow Race who would join them in their battle against their common enemy. The boys promised Lynn that no harm would come to her and she sincerely believed them, for they had been kind to her. After they had finished eating and drinking, Byron decided that they should stay and rest a little while longer before starting on their journey back to the city.

One full day had passed since the boys had been gone and Felicia and Byron's parents were already beginning to wonder and worry about them, hoping they would soon be back home. But, Billy had complete faith and told them so.

"The Great Spirit, Allestra, and Chief would safely get them home".

They had worked practically all day with Father Vincent enlisting the aid of as many people as they could to get them within the safety of the Church to pray together and break bread together as one family. They had been working tirelessly toward this goal but time would soon run out, for only one more day was left and they hoped and prayed it would not be the End. As Sara and Felicia had just about finished cleaning the kitchen, Sara turned to Felicia,

"God, I hope the boys are okay, but deep down I can't help feeling scared."

"I know how you feel Sara, because to tell you the truth, I'm scared too and I won't stop worrying until they're back home," answered Felicia.

"I keep telling myself to have faith, but I can't help wondering what they might run into out there".

Felicia then added, "You know, Sara, I'm so lucky to have you as my friend and I love you like a Sister". "You and your family have always been there for me when I needed help and I really thank you for that." Sara's face beamed with love and admiration as she looked at Felicia and hugged her.

"That was the most beautiful thing anyone has ever said to me, but I have to thank you too, for being my friend".

"Our families have been through so much together that I can't imagine us ever being without one another."

This time Angella happily skipped down the pathway that lead into the cavern, for she was going to visit her very own Archangel, and it was plain to see that Angella was becoming very attached to Allestra. Today, Allestra was carrying her staff and dressed as she was when Angella had first seen her, but her skin color kept changing and now it was a light shade of rose. As Allestra lovingly greeted the little girl, Angella asked her,

"Your skin color is different again today, but its always so beautiful".

"Why is it a different color"?, she asked.

Allestra's reply was only that,....

"Soon I prepare for battle".

"Come now, Angella, let us talk".

As Allestra finished the last word, she suddenly jerked her head and her eyes quickly moved from side to side, for her acute senses told her that He was there in the passageway, and she knew she must protect Angella. Allestra slapped her wrists together and as each wrist band met, a shocking swirl of crystal particles rapidly flowed to a corner in the cavern.

"Angella", she said, "Run into the lights, NOW"

"Do as I command, for The evil comes".

"You will not be able to see him but you will hear his words, and DO NOT COME OUT for anyone, not even if I call to you."

"I will walk into the light only when he is gone".

"Obey me NOW".

Angella shook with fear as she ran into the safety of the crystals as Allestra had commanded, and the dazzling turquoise blue zircons and crystal particles soon enveloped her in their protective cocoon of warmth and love. Allestra's deep Amethyst eyes sent celestial streams of fuschia and purple rays to the ground, a length of 7 feet in front of her, and would be invisible to the Demon. As she stood waiting, she could smell the evil from hell approaching and a little boy of Angella's age walked into the cavern calling Allestra's name.

"Allestra! "Allestra"!, "Where are you"! "Angella has sent me"!

"Please talk to me Allestra"!

Allestra slowly moved forward and stood her ground as she faced the young boy.

"Who Art Thou, young child that knows Angella"?

"Oh, yes, you really are as beautiful as Angella told me", said the boy.

Allestra again asked him who he was.

"My name is Lucien."

Allestra then asked him

"What has Angella told you?"

Lucien moved closer toward Allestra and stepped within the demarcation line, as he proceeded to explain what Angella had told him.

"Well, he said "I go to school with Angella and she told the whole class about you and about the Waters, and how you showed them to her."

"What else did she tell you Lucien", quiered Allestra?

"She said that only an Archangel could touch the Waters, but that maybe you would show me the waters as you showed her".

"I cannot show you the waters, for Satan may be lurking and he may contaminate them." And, what else would you like to know, Lucien"?

Lucien then smiled and turned his boyish eyes toward the great angel as he spoke

"Well, Is it not true that an Archangel cannot lie?"

"Yes that is true as it is ordained above, for no angel of God can lie," she said.

The little boy took a few more steps toward Allestra, hoping to get closer to her, but she retreated slowly as she spoke.

"Do not come closer to me, for I must not be touched, as I am preparing for battle."

Lucien then deviously asked.

"Battle"? "Battle with Whom"?

Allestra's voice powerfully echoed through the Cavern,

"Battle With You, Lucien, Beast of Hell." "Leave this holy place."

Satan transformed himself back into the handsome man from his first visit of temptation. Darting within and edged in purple, his horrific black eyes told the story of who he was. His thin lips were colorless and his tongue was dark and stained by sin.

"Does thou think thou art above Jesus?"?

"Does thou think that I cannot tempt thee?"

"Give me thy Water and we shall not join in battle".

As his unholy voice filled the cavern, Allestra glanced in the direction of the ground. From the ground, 7 enormous pillars of swirling purple flames towered into the air surrounding Satan. The Giant Pillars arched their flames 7 feet above Satan, sealing him under the pinnacles of the royal fires. Satan yelled like a wounded animal caught in a trap, for he knew that these were the "Gates of Hell". They were unbearable, for whenever he was forced to pass through them, he was branded with God's words spoken by Michael the Archangel who was Guardian of the "Gates of Hell". The Holy words caused great agonizing and burning pain that seared his flesh, his mind, and his evil soul. Since the creation of mankind, he has had to pass through the gates when he wished to come upon the earth and ravage humanity, and as powerful as he was, he could not change this. This is only one of the reasons Satan needed many souls to add to his damnation, for he would send his evil slaves in his place upon the earth to do his bidding and they would feel the agonizing pain. But, this time he had to come upon the earth himself because the Waters of Creation were too important for him to rely on his Slaves in Hell. He covered his ears as the voice and words brought him great anguish and the pains of Hell. "I am Michael, the Archangel who speaks God's Words and guards the Gates of Hell.

The voice continued.."God is Perfect". "God is Light.. "In The Beginning God Created..... ".

Satan yelled in anger and agony as he felt the searing pain of the Words in his soul. He deviously called to Angella mimicking Allestra's voice
"Angella, Angella, Help me".
"Help your Archangel".
Angella held her hands over her ears hoping to block out the cry for help, not knowing if it were really Allestra or the Evil One. It took all of the strength within her to fight the feeling of wanting to help her Allestra, but she kept telling herself to stay where she was and remembered what Allestra had told her, as Satan continued calling for Angella's help in a tortured and moaning voice. Allestra raised her eyes upward as she spoke in an unknown language and when she was finished, the purple "Gates of Hell" were gone and so was Lucien.

Hatred consumed his spirit and the pains of his evil echoed throughout with each deep and labored breath he took, as Satan's black soul bounded through the Gates of Hell into his domain of eternal damnation. He entered the confines of his kingdom which was a realm of torment with no light or mercy, and he was then cloaked in Hell's unholy mist of unnatural darkness. Deep purple fragments flickered through and around the black iris of his eyes as he cursed Allestra for he knew she would be formidable in battle, but he was sure he would defeat her and her God; the same God he had been waging war against since the beginning of time, for he had the scars of battle to prove it. The thought of waging War against the OTHER brought back the memory of the vow that he made when he dipped his golden eternal ring into the Black/Red waters of the River Carnage, within Hell's epicenter, many eons ago. Satan smugly smiled to himself as he looked down and fondled the once-golden ring on his finger, for he felt proud and delighted in the fact that He had created the "Ring of Fire" below the earth's crust causing earthquakes and eruptions of great magnitude and catastrophe to all mankind whenever and wherever he pleased. Again, he turned his evil mind toward Allestra and relished the thought of engaging in battle with her, crushing her into defeat, for nothing would stand in his way of owning the Holy Waters. And, there was also another reason he looked forward to this war against her and the OTHER, but that would have to wait until the great battle. He thought how it would give him great pleasure to completely destroy her, and then he toyed with the idea of an even greater pleasure he would derive in enslaving her soul which would surely drive a tumultuous spike into God's heart. Satan summoned his 4 generals; Kartos, Ravanu, Arachnon, and Saddesma who carried out his torturous commands and desires within the levels of his Hell. Their souls and eyes were like that of Satan, for they were part of his army who had been cast out with him from the House of God. As they entered his private level, only unearthly shadows could be seen of them, for they were also cloaked in the Demon's house of darkness and terror. In a voice filled with hate and jealousy, Satan commanded that they send Hemortus to stop the Yellow One from reaching Allestra-Terra, for he knew Allestra would gain even more power against him. Infallibly, he pronounced how he would be Mankind's absolute ruler and promised hideous torture for eternity to any that defied his will or refused to bow down to him. He promised his four Generals they would be greatly rewarded in all manner of unspeakable horror and lustful desires toward their human captives for eternity's ring of fire. They eagerly agreed and made their plans to wage their ultimate unholy battle for Satan's undeniable supremacy and pleasure. While no human could see him as long as he wished to stay invisible, Hemortus watched the three humans as they slept under the shade and protection of the large ledges. Hemortus had been given the command to kill the Yellow One and he must obey, for he feared what Satan would do to him if he failed. Hemortus silently crept down the side of the boulders as he inched closer to where they slept. Deviously, he would destroy their drinking water so they would become weakened by the steaming kiss of the sun's rays on their bodies and then he would hunt them down. Chief was ever watchful and could smell evil in the air. He raised his massive head and ears in defiance as his large jaws widened to reveal his huge canine teeth. With his upper lips perched in fierce anger and defense, he viciously growled as salvia slowly dripped down one side of his mouth. Sam and Byron jumped up simultaneously and as Sam looked at Chief, he caught a glimpse of the reflection of evil mirrored in Chief's eyes. Hemortus hadn't planned on a dog giving him any problems and Hemortus clawed the rocks as he quickly scampered back up the ledges, but not before he had broken open one of the bags of water. Sam was in shock at the evil he had just seen and remembered Allestra's words that they would see the face of evil. Byron had his knife in his hand ready to defend, but could see nothing and Lynn was so terrified that she backed herself into a crevice, fearful to venture out from beneath the ledge. Chief moved closer to Sam and Byron, as he intensely growled, warning this evil beast that he would protect and defend the three humans to the death. Hemortus knew that he must get rid of the dog first and then the rest would be easy. Sam couldn't get over the hideous beast he had just seen through Chief's eyes, for it was wretched, disfigured, and totally inhuman. It glared with evil and terror in its soul-less eyes and Sam shuddered as he tried to shake the awful image from his mind.

"Well, whatever it was, it got one of the bags of water, so I think we better leave now before it comes back", Byron stated.

"I saw it, Byron". "It was the most horrible and tortured thing I have ever seen."

"We have to stay close and protect Lynn."

The boys knew what it wanted, but were afraid to scare Lynn anymore than she already was. Chief had finally calmed down but was still standing his ground as the three of them gathered their things and combined what was left of the food into one bag. Byron decided that Sam would carry the food and water so he would be left free to fight with his knife. They would all walk together with Lynn between them while Chief would hold the front position. Sam bent down and patted Chief on his massive head,

"You're so courageous, My dear friend." "We're going to be okay, Chief."

"Just get us back to the Circle and we'll all be okay."

As Sam stood, he heard a voice in his mind that sounded like his Dad. Could it be, he thought, that Billy was communicating with him. Sam then concentrated to mentally listen as Billy spoke to him again.

"Sam, save the water you have left for as long as you can".

"Along the way there will be many plants and cactus that will help you survive".

"Cut them open and suck out the juices".

"They will be bitter, but will help all of you survive and use the water only when you really need it".

Sam then answered his father through his mind.

"Yes Father, I will."

Billy sat in his wheelchair in the Great Cathedral telling himself that he had faith in God and in Allestra. He was sure that Allestra would help the three return safely and he didn't care if he ever walked again, as long as all of them returned unharmed. With these thoughts in his mind, Billy stared at the statue of Allestra and saw that she was in full battle dress and looked completely pieced together except for one thing; the bird's talons sitting on her shoulder still did not have a body. It was very early on the second day and many people had already begun to gather onto the Church grounds and into the Cathedral. Father Vincent was preparing the altar and Joe was helping to organize some of the people who had come to the Church for refuge and tomorrow's meal. Felicia and Sara were in the basement helping the other woman with the preparation of the food for this monumental task. As Father Vincent finished preparing the altar, Billy's eyes were fixed upon the statue and his faith was undaunted, for he could feel it generating immense power, goodness, and love. Even though they were not too far from the city, they still had quite a way to go, for the journey was an arduous one considering the air was stifling as the unforgivable hot rays of the sun beat down upon them, stealing their energy. Sam remembered what his father had said to him about gaining nourishment from the many cacti that grew profusely in the area. They had already stopped a couple of times to eat a bit of their food and to also quench their thirst from the bitter cactus along the way. As they approached the end of a large bend in the road, they finally saw the outer edges of the Circle of Eternal Life as it loomed in the distance. At last it was within their view, and Sam felt a little more confident now, hoping they would soon reach it safely. Byron looked around very cautiously before deciding to stop for a brief moment because he realized Lynn really needed to rest. Byron and Sam quietly looked at each other and even though they were very glad at seeing the Circle of Eternal Life, they were still fearful of what they may have to face, for they knew that evil was out there somewhere just waiting for the right time to strike. Sam looked down at the dry, parched earth as he tried to imagine what it must have been like when it was green and fertile, when it supported food crops and the many animals who had once grazed there many years ago. He thought how much he loved this mother earth and all of the animals that had depended on her plentiful bounty. Byron could tell that Lynn was apprehensive about returning to the city where most of the people were prejudiced against her Race, for they blamed all of the Yellow Race for what had befallen the world. Byron reassured her that he would do the best he could to protect her and would never let any harm come to her. Lynn knew that she and her unborn child would have surely died from being exposed to the cruel elements if Byron and Sam had not come along when they did. They were different and she told herself to believe their story of the Archangel, for she hoped that maybe someday all people would soften their hearts to build a better New World where there would be no prejudice and where everyone would get along, no matter what color they were. As they rested, Sam pulled out the jug of water for the first time since they had started their journey back to the city. "Here, I think we could all use a little of this now, but we still have to be careful not to waste it."

He then handed the jug to Lynn.

"Just take a little sip to wet your lips and quench your thirst."

As Lynn looked at Sam, she nodded her head in an affirmative and appreciating manner, to say Thank You. When Lynn finished drinking, she passed the jug to Byron and he took a quick swig of water, wiped his mouth with his arm, and then handed the jug back to Sam. After Sam had his drink of water, he called Chief over and gave him a drink of the precious fluid. As Chief finished slurping the water, he shook the dust off of his body and flicked his large tongue over his lips and nose, and a few drops of water hit the parched ground. A snake had crawled out from beneath a rock sensing the water of life, but Chief was in his way and the snake coiled itself as it sent out its feared death rattle of warning. Lynn screamed and ran toward Byron, as Sam calmly held Chief and told him not to move. He then slowly inched his way between Chief and the Snake's position, as the Snake reared its head higher while it's high pitched rattle pierced the silence. Sam calmly bent down and looked at the Snake while he spoke to it with his eyes and mind.

"Go back under the shelter of the rocks, for it is only there that you will be safe and unharmed. You must be patient just a little while longer, for the creator has promised that soon there will be plenty of water for you and all of His creatures."

The snake listened to the language of these words within its mind, and understanding them, he cautiously lowered his head and then slid back to the safety of the rocks. A look of respect and admiration for what Sam had just done, shown brightly in Byron's eyes and in his words as he approached Sam.

"I've always thought of you as a kid and when we left on this journey, I still thought of you as a Kid, but you're also my friend";

"Now, you're more than that, little brother".

Byron paused and then said

"You are a True Apache Warrior."

These were the words that Sam had dreamed of hearing some day, and now that they had been spoken, Sam was completely speechless, for these words were a great honor and they meant that he was no longer thought of as a child. Byron smiled as he looked at Sam, for he could see the illuminating glow of manhood in Sam's eyes, and then he playfully punched Sam's arm.

"We better get moving now, We'll be safe once we cross into the Circle of Eternal Life."

Hemortus thought to himself as he watched this frail human behavior, that he, himself, had once been a human being which seemed an eternity ago. It was so very long ago that he could just barely remember; or was it that the pangs of these human memories brought great anguish to his soul, knowing that he was but an empty shell now, with Satan as his master for all of Hell's eternity. If Satan knew that Hemortus was even thinking, he would punish and cruelly torture him as he had many times in the past. Hemortus quickly turned his thoughts toward his plan and the reason he was sent to do Satan's bidding. Sam had given him an idea and he would strike when they least expected it.

Angella and Allestra sat protected within the magnificent colored prisms of sparkling emerald, ruby, and sapphire hues along with twinkling rays of Blue Zircons and pure heavenly crystals that surrounded them in God's World of indescribable feelings of love and warmth.

"This will be a very important lesson for you to learn, Angella, for this is the last time you will be alone with me."

It upset Angella to hear these words. With her beautiful and innocent eyes, Angella looked at Allestra "Please, I don't want you to ever leave me, what would I do?"

"After the battle, I must return, but I will be with you in spirit and watch over you always."

"Your grandmother loves you very much and she has been a kind, and loving mother to you, for she has guided you well to choose the path which leads to God's glorious home where you will truly live someday." "When that time draws near, I will be there for you at the end of your long journey, as I will also be there for Sam and Byron, for This is a very great and special Honor that God bestows on you and your friends." "Then, I will really see you again; Oh, I can't wait, because I miss you already," Angella retorted in her adorable fashion.

Allestra then told Angella,

"It will be a very long time yet, for you have much more to learn than I can teach you now".

"You must listen and learn from your grandmother, for she is very wise and caring".

"Are you going to come for my grandmother and Billy too"?

"Yes, little one, but their time has not yet come", answered Allestra.

"They will not be alone, but now, we must begin your lesson" "Your knowledge will be vast and unmatched, for Sam, Byron and many others will turn to you for truth and advice."

Angella asked, "But what will I do when my Grandmother is gone?"

"Where will I find the answers, and what will I do when I'm afraid.?"

Allestra bent her head and gently looked into Angella's questioning eyes and responded.

"Beloved, this is the great lesson that I will teach you."

"You already have the answers and strength within you."

Angella listened in awe and anticipation as she clung to every word Allestra spoke.

"God created all of us with a great power that lies within every soul, for it is instilled at the time of birth". "All of the strength and power you will ever need is within you, for you are a Circle of Eternal Life within yourself".

"You must search for it within and you will find it, for it is there for you to draw upon, just as you drew upon it when the Beast called out to you."

Angella listened to the power of Allestra's words and then asked.

"Why are there bad, evil people if we all have the same power within us?"

Allestra explained to her that

"These people were not born evil, but became greedy for money and power, and looked for the easy path to the riches, glory, and material things of this earth".

"They were swayed by the voice of Satan, for he promised to give them all they craved and he whispered all that they wanted to hear". "So, they did not search for the truth and strength within themselves, and did not help their fellow man".

"They knowingly betrayed all good things for their wills were free to choose, but they chose corruption, disobedience, dishonored life, stealing, lying, cheating, deceitfulness, hatred, and Murder."

"By these deeds, they sealed their fate with Satan to attain their unholy goals, not caring or thinking about the riches of a greater life in God's Heart and House."

"They lived only for their day on earth, not believing they would spend an eternity in Hell, and their once pure souls became dismal and dark with evil and hatred toward all the colors of mankind".

"Due to Greed, many in high places of power betrayed their people's trust in them and because of this, mankind lived and died through great wars, and has suffered much as have all creatures created by the Lord". "Throughout the ages, evil people have caused millions to perish and cared not of the human misery and suffering inflicted onto their fellow man and all creatures of the earth because they follow Satan's ways."

"As long as they were not hungry",

"As long as their children were not poisoned with the pollution of the fragile earth and its wonderous creatures,"

"As long as they and their children were not homeless"

"As long as they had power, money, and great fortune; They were above all";

"They forgot that they are not above God, who is their one and only Judge".

"They forgot that God is above Satan and all of Infinity"

"They forgot to Worship God and instead worshiped Satan."

"They did not listen to their hearts and they closed their eyes not caring to know or realize that even Satan Fears God, for Satan knows that God has no equal."

"And, they forgot who God is, for He is the One absolute and infinitely perfect spirit who is the creator of all."

"So, Angella, when you feel lost and need help, gather the gift of strength and light within you and listen to its voice, for it is God speaking to you".

"It is God mending You". "It is God showing you the way".

"Follow it, Feel it, for you will never be alone as He is with you on the True Path."

Angella was mesmerized by Allestra's Words and instilled them in her mind and heart, never to be forgotten. "Your grandmother waits for you now." said Allestra.

"I wish I didn't have to leave yet; "Will, (Angella hesitated) "Will I see you tomorrow?", she asked.

"Yes, Angella, You will see me again tomorrow when Sam and Byron bring the Yellow One to me".

Angella walked through the cavern thinking about all that she had learned this day.

She then stopped and turned to look back at Allestra standing in the rays of God's light and yelled out to her. "Allestra, Great Archangel created by God";

"I love you and Most of all, I love God for sending you to me."

As Angella turned out of the great cavern and into the passageway, she had no way of knowing that an Archangel could ever shed a tear, as a tear drop of light Amethyst gently slid down the golden face of an angel.

Hemortus laid his ashen gray body face down on the ground in a prone position with his arms and hands held tightly against his sides. Within a moment, he turned into a slithering mottled small brown snake with a killing venom unrivaled by any other known to man. He must soon catch up to the group of humans to accomplish his mission, for they were not that far away from the Circle of Eternal Life. Billy wrenched in horror as his mind saw the evil plot unfold and tried to contact Sam with his mind, but something was interfering and he couldn't seem to get through no matter how hard he tried. Billy felt exhausted and powerless, but prayed to God and hoped that Allestra would help them. As they got closer to the Circle of Eternal Life, Chief's gait turned from a walk into his proud prance, happily wagging his tail and barking, as if telling his friends that they would soon be home. Out of nowhere, silent and deadly, Hemortus struck Chief's front leg with a viscous fang and deposited his deadly venom into the valiant Dog's blood stream. As Chief yelped out in pain, Hemortus unlocked his jaws and quickly slithered away and Sam screamed out in horror, running toward his fallen dog, lying there dying. Byron and Lynn ran to Sam as all three of them cried, but none cried more than Sam. He tried to choke back the tears, but couldn't.

"Please Allestra, Don't let Chief die." "Please Save him."

Chief looked at Sam one last time before his eyes glazed over, as his tongue was quickly losing its pink color, and Chief knew he was dying. Sam held Chief's head in his lap and as tears rolled down Sam's face, he said to Chief.

"We grew up together you and I". "You were always there for me, loyal to the end".

"When I cried, you made me laugh, and when I needed you, you protected me."

"And now I can't save you."

Chief's eyes were glazed over and lifeless now as his tongue turned dark with death. Byron and Lynn could not speak for they felt a deep ache in their hearts for both Sam and Chief. With a lump in his throat, Sam gently lowered Chief's noble head to the ground and slowly got up.

"I didn't know how much it could hurt to be a true Apache warrior."

Byron could see the sorrow in Sam's eyes and face, and he knew that no words could ever console his friend. After a moment in silence, Byron then gently said,

"Come on Sam, You know we gotta leave his body".

"We can't take him back with us now and we don't even have

the time to bury him".

"We gotta cross over right away, before that THING comes back for the rest of us."

Sam nodded his already lowered head for he knew Byron was right, but Sam also knew that this evil thing killed Chief first, for it knew Chief would protect them and in Sam's mind, this thing was nothing but a coward. Tears of grief and relief fell down Sam's face as they crossed into the Circle of Eternal Life. Now they only had 7 more miles to go, but at least they were safe because Chief had given up his life for them. Allestra knew what Hemortus had done and she also knew that he would not stop with killing Chief, for Chief was only his first kill and with the dog out of the way, he could now go after his real target, the yellow one, even if it meant crossing into the Circle of Eternal Life. She knew that Sam and Byron would let their guard down now, for they had no idea that Hemortus could cross over as they had done. Hemortus would have one earth hour of time within the circle before being cast out, but Allestra could not take the chance of leaving the three unprotected; for she knew Hemortus could kill all three of them within a matter of moments. Allestra-Terra raised her Staff toward the heavens and asked for God's infinite protection and help. She then commanded

"Caninus Lupus, Mother of all Wolves, come forth and bring with you the Great Mastiff, ancestor of the first seed to the Apollo of Dogs".

As their spirit forms appeared, she commanded them in the name of the Creator.

"Go forth and find thy Kind".

"Guard his body against all evil that may take it, for You will know what to do when you see the shadow."

The spirit dogs howled as they leaped through the air and ran across the desert lands toward Chief's body. Allestra pointed the pulsating deep Amethyst crystal to the ground, and before her, the Holy Waters of Creation bubbled up into a pool of rich life-giving Deep Amethyst waters. As she bent to touch them, she prayed aloud

"Dear Magnificent Creator of all Mankind, of all Life on earth, and in the eternal Universe of thy Great Heavens; Thou art the only ONE who can create from thy Holy Water."

She ran her fingers through the royal blue and purple waters and a light purple mist appeared hovering over the waters as she touched them. Allestra continued....

"The Holy Waters are the Waters of Thy Creation from the beginning to eternity. From them, Your hands have created all of the greatest wonders of the Worlds." "Dominus, Create again and give back thy wondrous Sky to the Creature of all the Heavens, so that Aquila may fly in your Grace and Honor you with the Heavens above him and the Earth below his wings; where once again, he will sing his song of sweet praises to your Holy Name".

As Allestra praised God's power, the soft mist formed a pair of birds talons that soon rested upon her shoulder, and with each word she spoke in reverence to the Almighty Giver of Life; Aquila, the Majestic Bald Eagle, with its lofty and incomparable wing span was brought forth upon the earth again. The purity of his white feathers covered his powerful but regally arched head and neck. His eyes were sharp and alive with the keenest vision above all other birds. He was complete perfection, for no other bird commanded and ruled the skies as he did. Allestra bowed in thanks to God for his most Perfect Creation. She then filled a small waxen flask with precious drops of the Holy Waters and tied the flask around the Great Bird's Neck as the Eagle looked into Allestra's eyes and knew what was expected of him. In all of his glory and power, the great Eagle spread his wings and spiraled upward directly toward the Heavens, first thanking God for creating him to fly the skies once more. He then extended his powerfully arched wings through the air, as he swiftly soared over the edge of the great lake and across the desert lands toward Chief's Body. Billy leaned his head backward and closed his eyes, for his mind had been there with Allestra as thoughts of her statue flashed before him. "I should have known it could only have been a Great Eagle, honored spirit of my ancestors." She was almost complete, Billy thought to himself. He knew without a doubt that the boys would return safely with the Yellow One and then Allestra would be whole to enforce God's Will, for she was an Archangel, an Almighty Warrior of the Lord. Hemortus stood before the Circle of Eternal Life gazing at its wondrous colors. He thought to himself that this would be the closest he would ever get to seeing the face of the OTHER. He could not speak HIS name, nor dare even to think HIS name, for Satan would wreak his revenge on him in the eternity of Hell's evil grip. Hemortus knew that if he crossed over, he would not have much time before he would be cast out and he was afraid of the consequences, for he feared Satan's punishment more; and this thought instilled absolute terror into his dark, enslaved, lifeless soul. Once the spirit dogs approached Chief's body, they circled it 7 times as they howled in grief for one of their own. Lupus, Mother of Wolves, took her position 4 feet away from Chief's head, while the Great Mastiff stood his ground 3 feet from Chief's flank. The two great spirit dogs sent their resounding warning shrieks up toward the sky, telling all living and dead that they protect this ground and the carcass that lies upon it, as vigilantly, they waited for the sign from their Great Master. From above, the Supreme Eagle looked down with his pin-point vision of impeccable accuracy, encompassing all beneath him and the objective within. The majestic eagle circled the area, and as he flew lower and lower, his magnificent wing span cast a shadow upon the ground. The ancestor spirit dogs inched away from Chief's body acknowledging the Great Bird of Prey to come closer. As the eagle glided a little lower, he swooped down to the precise spot and hovered 3 feet in the air over Chief's Body. His powerful talons were spread open and the strength of his wings flapped in the air to hold his position, while he pierced open the wax-encased Waters of Creation with his beak of steel. The great bird continued hovering over Chief until the precious fluid had been dispersed onto Chief's Body. When Aquila was finished, he let out his call of accomplishment as he flapped his wings of wind upward into the heavens above for his return to Allestra. The eagle was soon out of sight and the two spirit dogs waited patiently for Chief to rise; and as they watched and waited, God's creation of life took hold. Chief's front legs and paws twitched with movement as his large, benevolent eyes slightly opened while his tongue became pink with color again and he whimpered as his tail slowly began to thump the ground; and the spirt dogs approached him, calling to him, entreating him to rise up. With renewed life, Chief pulled his massive body up and took a stance of power with his head held high and ears erect, for the two spirit dogs beckoned him to run with them to the Circle of Eternal Life. He answered their call with complete passion and devotion, for the "Apollo of Dogs" knew that he must protect Sam and the others from the evil menace that stalked them. Hemortus still hesitated at crossing into the Circle of Eternal Life. Once more, he turned his head to look behind him and in the distance, he could see Chief running like a steed covering an enormous amount of ground, and soon the great dog would be upon him. At that moment, Hemortus knew he must cross over and without further delay, he entered through the vertical sheaths of the Circle of Eternal Life. He must find them before the dog did, for Hemortus knew that he would not be able to kill the animal again, for this time it was protected with a spiritual life unto its own. As he walked within the circle, Hemortus felt strange. He thought

"Is it that I have a conscience"?.

"Do I still have a heart even though my soul is no longer mine".?

He told himself do not think of such things and he reminded himself what he was there to do, as he was damned to hell and dared not to even think of betraying Satan, for Satan would put flesh back on his body only to be painfully ripped off, time and time again. As they reached the top of a knoll, Sam, Byron, and Lynn finally had the city close within their view and as they looked around the knoll, they saw a very old man sitting out in the open elements, waiting to die as the elderly so often did. The old man looked very weak, maybe even dead, they thought. Lynn was exhausted carrying the baby within her and she needed this rest. Byron told her to stay where she was while he and Sam walked toward old man to investigate. From the top of the knoll, Byron and Sam could see in all directions, so they felt fairly safe in stopping here. The old man was barely alive, hoping to die quickly now, and Sam wet the old man's mouth with some of the water while Byron motioned to Lynn to join them. Lynn shared some water with Byron and Sam, as the old man closed his eyes in the sweltering heat of the sun. As Chief leaped through the Divine sheaths of the Circle, his two spirit guides joined forces and leaped within him, making Chief one with his great ancestors. He raced after the scent of his master with the speed of a cheetah and the heart of a valiant lion. Hemortus knew that all he had to do to satisfy Satan was to kill the yellow one. The two boys didn't matter to him unless they got in his way, but he must do this quickly before the earth-hour was up. He still had plenty of time left, so he would be patient, for as far as they were concerned, he was just an old man ready to die. Hemortus thought that he would wait a few minutes and then call the girl to him begging her to wipe the sweat from his brow so as to make him more comfortable before dying, and then he would strike swiftly. The strange feeling of consciousness came over Hemortus again and he wondered how many more times must he kill, how many more times must he appease Satan? If only there was a way out, but there was no hope for him and Hemortus struggled with these thoughts as he called to Lynn. The old man weakly motioned to her.

"Please girl, please grant an old man's dying wish".

"Please wipe my face and talk to me before I die.", he spoke.

Lynn took the water jug with her as Byron and Sam looked around the knoll for the evil stalking them, not knowing it had already been there waiting. She gently wiped his forehead and spoke with him and told him of the Archangel who was to do battle with Satan so the World could be saved. Hemortus could hardly stand to hear these soft spoken words, for he so longed to be one of them, to be free again, and to have a second chance at life. He quickly grabbed her tightly by the throat but hesitated, just holding her throat so she could not move; and Byron seeing this, ran to her defense trying to stab the old man, when suddenly the old man stood up as Hemortus.

Hemortus still had his grey lifeless hands around Lynn's neck telling Byron

"Your knife cannot kill me, for I am already dead."

Byron and Sam stood motionless, pleading with Hemortus not to kill Lynn.

"I must kill the yellow one".

"I must obey Satan, for he will torture me beyond your wildest dreams."

Just as Hemortus finished speaking, Chief leaped from out of nowhere onto the back of Hemortus and knocked him down to the dusty, parched ground as he lunged upon Hemortus with the fierceness of his barred teeth, ripping at his face, neck, and whole body. Then in a split second as if Chief had been commanded, he stopped and backed away from Hemortus, still growling in fierce anger. Sam, Byron, and Lynn were in a state of shock at all that had transpired and even though they were afraid, Sam's heart beat with happiness and amazement at the site of the beloved dog that he was sure he would never see again. The despair in Hemortus' voice could be heard as he slowly stood up.

"I wish I could really die to never know that I had lived, to truly die so as not to feel the pain of darkness." "Satan enslaves my condemned soul for eternity and I will dearly pay the price of his hideous hatred, anger, and torture now forever, for Satan despises Mankind and wants our souls, in the hope of destroying the OTHER."

The three of them could hardly look upon this doomed creature, Hemortus, but felt pangs of sorrow for him at the same time, for once he was human as they. Allestra-Terra's voice answered Hemortus, but she was nowhere to be seen.

"I speak to you, Hemortus, as an Archangel of the Lord." "Yes, it is true you are condemned to Hell for your vile acts against mankind, for when you did these horrible deeds, you struck your hand against the Lord who created you." "You had many chances during your life to change your ways, but you refused to hear God's voice". "Instead, you listened to Satan's corrupt and empty promises in exchange for your soul, but you did not realize what it would mean to live in Hell's eternity with the Monster." The pain and suffering in Hemortus's voice could be heard as he spoke.

"Archangel, why do you speak to me now"?
"Do you not know what I face since I have failed".?
Allestra answered.
"You failed because you hesitated." "You, I, and God knows that you could have killed her instantly with one stroke of your hand; but you did not, even though you know what awaits you in Hell when Satan hears of your betrayal."

"What will I do now, Archangel, for there is no mercy or hope for me", he answered.

"I cannot judge thee Hemortus, for only God has the right to do so, but through His words to me, He brings the promise of special Hope to you." "At the great battle, you will be tested and that is all that I can say." "But, when I return to Hell, Satan will know that I have not killed the yellow one, and he will read my mind and soul and know I have spoken to you.", said Hemortus.

Allestra asked Byron to cut a lock of Lynn's hair and hand it to Hemortus.

"You will bring this lock of hair with you to prove to Satan that you committed the deed and when he reads your soul, he will see this is true, for you will have this memory in your mind and soul when he searches it." "The hour is now at hand to take thy place in Hell."

In an instant, Hemortus disappeared before their very eyes as if he never existed, and Allestra then spoke to Byron, Sam, and Lynn.

"You are safe now and All evil is gone until the battle."
Allestra's voice then faded as she told them,

"When you reach the Cathedral, you will need rest and nourishment; then I will call you."

Lynn was no longer afraid and for the first time she felt safe. Byron gathered what was left of the food and water and spoke to Sam.

"We made it, Apache Warrior, but I'm really nervous about this battle tomorrow, not knowing what to expect".

"You know I'm not afraid of anything and I know Allestra is powerful, but the words of Hemortus sent chills through me, brother."

"I know, Sam said; His words were just as terrifying as he looked, but We can't lose with God and Allestra by our side". "Look, they brought Chief back to me alive and well". "We all saw him dead, you know that." "Only God could have brought him back." "Only God", Sam repeated, as he lovingly embraced his loyal dog and gave him a tidbit of food and some water.

Byron and Lynn smiled at Chief and agreed that..

"Yeah. "Only God can do such things."

Byron then added, "Come on, we'll be there in no time if we leave now."

They rambled down the knoll to the final path leading toward the city with renewed energy and excitement at the thrill of reaching their destination. At Sam's side, Chief pranced with power and dignity telling the earth who he was

"Apollo of Dogs, Faithful Creature of the Lord",

protecting the future generations and hopes of the world, guiding them all back home.

CHAPTER 4

No-one, not even his Generals, dare enter this sequestered chamber within his level, where Satan often went to be alone with his evil thoughts, for this was his own private place in Hell where he would bring forth the evil from his mind onto the world. This private chamber is where he appeased himself with all that he desired within his domain of eternal damnation, knowing that he now held the ultimate power over all of the souls within his confines which had once belonged to God, and this brought him great joy. His cruel eyes scanned the black and gray bedrock with short piercing purple rays as if searching for something from long ago. His search ended as his rays locked-on to the tarnished silver & golden wrist bands. One wrist band had three large stones which included two 6 carat diamonds and one 6 carat deep unholy Amethyst stone that sat between the diamonds. They had been presented to him millions of earth years ago, but now they had become just as evil as he, for they had taken on and absorbed all of his evil properties and energy within them, just as the other wrist band which carried a 10 carat black diamond surrounded by rows of gray lifeless crystals and once-deep blue, sparkling zircons, but before going into Battle he would cast his spell on them to give them a false brilliance and unrivaled power, to even Allestra's gems. As Satan looked at the wrist bands, he became enraged as he spoke

"You shall see and feel my merciless power when we join in battle".

Satan then angrily left his chamber room furious with thoughts of jealousy and vengeance on his mind. As his tortured soul painfully brushed through the agonizing gates of hell, Satan's powerful mind and will compelled Hemortus to his level. Satan's eyes pierced the unholy darkness leering at the captive soul before him and still seething in anger toward thoughts of Allestra, Satan questioned Hemortus and asked.

"Hast Thou obeyed my Command"?

In a meek and terrified voice, the soul of Hemortus answered the question.

"Yes, Great Master of Darkness, I have done what you have commanded of me."

Satan sneered as he relished the thought of torturing his captive prey if he were to catch him lying to him. "What Proof do you have that I may know the Yellow One is no longer."

As Satan asked this question, his intense will pulled the captive soul a little closer to him.

"I have brought you a lock of the Yellow one's hair, so that you would know she is dead, for I only had one earth hour within the Circle and did not have the time to bring more of her body to you, as the Dog beast protected with new life, swiftly stalked me.", replied Hemortus.

With uncanny quickness and speed, Satan visciously grabbed the hair from Hemortus, felt it, smelled it, and examined each strand very carefully to confirm it had belonged to one of the Yellow Race. His wild and evil voice pierced the air as he summoned his Generals. Hemortus was still under Satan's grip of scrutiny and could not freely leave until Satan was thoroughly satisfied. Satan sneered in delight as he told his Generals that the Circle of Eternal Life had been cast around the City where they would do battle, and how he would cast his ring of fire and darkness to pierce the Circle, for Satan was sure that he and his army would destroy Allestra-Terra and seize the water. He then turned his sinister black and purple eyes toward Hemortus, and in front of his Generals, he spoke.

"Hemortus has killed the Yellow One and because thou has obeyed me, thou shall join us in the Great Battle."

Hemortus bowed in allegiance to the evil one as Satan's grip on his soul loosened ever so slightly.

"Yes, Satan, Hemortus answered."

As Hemortus took a small step backward, Satan surprised him with the force and speed of his powerful mind and will, drawing Hemortus ever so much tighter and closer, as Satan spoke in a lecherous tone.

"Hemortus, Did thou think that I would forget and let thee go before searching every corner of thy mind and dark soul"?

"For, if I find a gnat of light, thou shall be condemned even further below and thou shall spend 1000 earth years chained to the "Gates of Hell" to feel their pain without mercy or relief."

Satan's cruel eyes sent prying black and purple rays searching the mind and helpless soul of Hemortus, looking for a speck of light to expose him as a traitor, but Satan could find none and only then did he believe Hemortus. As Satan released his willful grip on Hemortus, he commanded him to return to the third level until he would be called again. Satan then turned his attention toward his generals as they began planning for the battle.

Christians, Moslems, Jews, Hindus, and families of all faiths and color joined Father Vincent in prayer to thank God for the food they were about to eat, and although their religious beliefs differed, they were true believers in God's power and grace, and felt safe on the grounds of this House of God, for their own houses of worship had been destroyed and this was a safe haven for them until they could rebuild their own Temples to God. When Father Vincent finished his blessing over the food, he asked them to join him in prayer for the safe return of the boys with one of the Yellow Race. After the prayer, Rabbi Silverman stood up and said.

"Father Vincent, I speak not just as a Man of God to you, but as a dear friend".

"I want to say Thank You for all you have done for all of us, allowing us to share your Food and goodness, and opening your Cathedral to peoples of all faiths."

As Father Vincent thanked the Rabbi, he heard a Dog barking in the background and his heart skipped a beat for it sounded like Chief. All were quiet as the barking came nearer and nearer until into the Great Banquet Hall they marched, the four of them, like soldiers coming home from the Great Crusades. Sara and Felicia stopped in the middle of serving the food as they held their breaths and then ran toward them excited at seeing the boys safely home at last. Father Vincent embraced Lynn as if he had known her all of his life and Lynn was speechless at the warm feeling of love and acceptance.

Angella ran to Sam hugging him and said

"I've missed you so much, but I just knew you and Byron could do it, and I wasn't afraid because I knew Chief was there with you."

As Felicia ran up to Sam, Angella bent down and wrapped her arms around Chief's large neck, hugging and petting him, as Billy waited proudly and patiently to speak to his son, while Sara and Joe greeted Byron with tears in their eyes happy at his safe return. The congregation cheered and clapped while Sam approached his father and their eyes met knowing each other's thoughts, and Sam stood before his father as a Proud Apache Warrior would have; for the boy who left, had now returned as a man. Billy nodded at the young warrior before him, as Sam knelt beside his father and wrapped his arms around Billy's neck. Angella walked up to Lynn to make friends and ask her to sit at the table beside her, as Sara and Felicia made room for the gallant ones at the Banquet Table near Father Vincent. As the congregation enjoyed their meal, the boys told them about their journey and all that happened; how Chief had been bitten by evil and died, and then of his glorious return to life. The congregation listened intently and clung to every word when suddenly a voice like none other was heard in the Great Banquet Hall. They sat quietly as the voice grew louder, for it was Allestra speaking to them and her wonderous calming words filled the room.

"Do not be afraid for everyone that Believes in God shall be saved".

"Prepare yourselves in prayer this day to your God above, for tomorrow the battle begins against the treacherous enemy of God and of all Mankind, for by my oath, Satan shall not control God's Holy Waters of Creation."

Allestra then said

"Let the children rest from their long journey; then I will meet with them."

Her voice then faded into the distance,

"Have Faith, for the true believers of God will be saved."

There was complete silence in the Banquet Room as the people looked at each other in awe at hearing the voice of the Archangel; but because they were human, fear and anxiety could be seen in their eyes, yet in their hearts and souls they believed that their faith was all powerful, and as they left the room, they hugged each other and promised themselves to pray together as one family of mankind in the belief that God would protect them and save the World for all of God's children. By this time, Lynn, Byron, and Sam were feeling the effects of their long and emotional journey, and so was Chief. Lynn felt comfortable and safe being here with them, but most of all she felt truly accepted, relieved, and comforted knowing that her unborn child would have a chance in life, where she hoped that finally people of all races would make a truly sincere effort to get along and stop the hatred and prejudice in their hearts. As Lynn thought about these things, Angella took Lynn by the hand and led her to the wine cellar as if she were leading a sister; and as Lynn felt the warm, caring touch of Angella's little hand in hers, Lynn spoke with a sincere truth at what she was feeling at that moment.

"Angella, I feel as if I've known you all of my life, for I feel so very close to you".

"At the touch of your hand, it's as if you've taken away all of the tears, hurt, and anguish that I've felt for much too long."

As Angella looked up at Lynn's face with her adorable big laughing eyes and dimples on her cheeks, Lynn said to her.

"If my baby's a little girl, I hope she grows up to be just like you".

Lynn paused and then added "and would you mind, if I named

her Angella".?

Angella's eyes widened even more in surprise that she was almost speechless as she opened her lips into a very wide smile and excitedly said,

"Lynn, you really mean that, a little baby named after me.?"
"Oh! Yes Lynn, that would be just great, somebody named after me, she repeated". "Wait till my Grandmother hears this; she'll be so happy too."

Joe had rearranged the sleeping quarters of the wine cellar and Byron and Sam were already fast asleep on the one side of the room, with Chief snoring in the background. Angella and Lynn tiptoed in to the other side of the partition where their mats were set up, and they too soon fell fast asleep. Joe, Sara, and Felicia were helping the other workers clean up the banquet room and finishing their kitchen chores, so Billy was chosen to watch over the children and Lynn. In his wheelchair, Billy pushed himself into the room and glanced over the whole room to see that Lynn and Angella were safely sleeping, and as his eyes wandered over to the other side of the room, he looked at Byron and then toward his son, soundly sleeping, as a smile crossed his eyes and lips, for he was very grateful that they had safely returned, but deep in his heart he knew without a doubt that they had been chosen to fulfil a wonderous destiny. As Joe entered the room, he bent over and whispered to Billy

"That journey must have taken a lot out of them, Look, they're still sleeping."

"Yes, said Billy, but it's so good to have them back, isn't it"?

Joe answered "I know, I know, it sure is good".

"I really missed them but I'm so glad that they're safe now."

Sara and Felicia then entered the room to see that Angella and Lynn were soundly sleeping.

"That poor young girl".

"I don't know how she made the trip being pregnant".

"It must have really been hard on her.", said Sara.

Felicia then softly spoke so as not to wake them.....

"Yes, It took a lot of courage and faith, but I'm so glad she believed that Byron and Sam would not harm her."

"Sara, when do you think her baby is due?"

"She looks pretty far along don't you think?" Sara nodded in agreement

"You know I was just thinking that".

"From the looks of her I'd say she's at least 8 months along or maybe more."

Billy felt it was time for all of them to get some rest.

"We should all get a little rest now because I have a feeling this is going to be a very long night."

Joe agreed.

"Yeah, I think your're right Billy. "Only God knows what's ahead of us and we all have to be ready." Joe then sat down on the floor and leaned up against one of the walls, while Felicia and Sara laid down on their mats to take a quick nap. Father Vincent was in the inventory room looking at the dwindling supply of food. To anyone else's eyes, it looked as though they had plenty of food for everyone, but Vincent knew different. With more and more people looking toward him with hope, a place to stay, and a good meal, he knew the food supply would not last another 2 years as he had hoped, even with all that he had accomplished thus far, not to mention the water supply and the whole unnatural state the Earth was in. As he laid his inventory sheet down, he rested his forehead on one of the huge tall cartons stacked in a corner of the room.

"Dear God, have mercy on us." "Please don't let your children suffer anymore."

Allestra-Terra's words filled his inner self.

"Vincent, soon the time comes for new life."

"Bring the Yellow One and all of them to me now, even Sara, Joe, and Billy, for soon God's life and spirit will fill His Earth once more."

With Hope in his heart, Vincent answered

"Thank You Dear God, for I am your servant always."

Father Vincent entered the wine cellar and nudged Billy.

"Billy, he said, Allestra spoke to me and told me that the time has come."

"She wishes all of us, including Sara and Joe, and you to go to her now."

Billy's expression was one of excitement as he listened to what Father Vincent had just said.

"At last, I'm really going to see her".

What a great honor he thought.

"I'll wake Joe and the Boys, while you get the others up, said Vincent."

They were all awake now and Vincent told them.

"Come, it is time to go to Allestra, for she spoke to me and she wishes to see us."

They walked together through the fruit cellar and down the passageway that led to the cavern beneath the Church. Father Vincent led the way while Joe pushed Billy's wheelchair with Chief and Sam walking by Billy's side. Angella took Lynn by the hand as they followed behind Sam and Chief. "Don't be afraid Lynn", Angella said,

"You'll love Allestra as I do because she already loves you."

Lynn squeezed Angella's hand and took a deep breath. Felicia put her arm around Sara in happiness that she was taking her dear friend to meet the Beautiful Archangel, with Byron following closely behind them. As they turned the corner from the passageway into the Cavern, Allestra's heavenly glow could be seen in the distance waiting for them, and Billy's heart beat faster with anticipation as they drew nearer to her light. As they approached the light, Allestra stepped out and stood before them in all of her pure heavenly glory and power, and there were no adequate words to explain or describe what they saw or felt. As she stood before them, her skin was the warm color of bronze, gently kissed by the sun and her deep amethyst eyes, brows, and lashes were indescribably beautiful glowing against the color of her skin. As her golden/bronze hair flowed, a delicately woven headband of small white gardenia-type flowers graced her forehead, each studded with an Amethyst crystal at the core of each flower, and around her neck she wore the Amethyst star cross, sparkling in all of its rich passionate glory. Her sandals matched her white angelic toga and a shawl of heavenly fabric draped her left shoulder, holding the perched Great Bird of Prey. In her right hand she held the richly carved mahogany staff with the beautiful vibrant crystal for all to see and her wrists were wrapped in the glorious golden wrist bands covered with all the wonderous gems of God's Earth, as their dazzling colors flickered and danced like millions of fireflies. They stood before her in complete ecstasy at this glimpse of heaven before them. With no words spoken, Allestra-Terra raised her left arm out in front of her body and shook her wrist back and forth several times. As she did this, particles of gemstars of every color flowed and musically chimed from her wrist band, encircling the cavern. In unison, they formed a heavenly reflection of twinkling prisms of gem-dust colors, singing their enchanting melody while enveloping the cavern and all within. Allestra-Terra then spoke.

"I have much to speak to you about and we are now protected by God's light for Satan cannot pierce it and listen to what I must tell you."

As Allestra-Terra spoke, she called upon

"Lynn, daughter of God's Yellow Race, Come forth with the innocent child that you carry."

Angella nodded to Lynn as if to tell her, do not be afraid. As Lynn walked out a few steps from the rest of the group, Allestra asked the question.

"Beautiful Daughter of the Yellow Race, Do you stand with God and your brothers, against Satan?".

Lynn stood in front of Allestra and looked up at her brilliant purple eyes

"Yes, Allestra, My child and I both stand before God and with him always, against all that is evil."

A smile crossed Allestra's face as the vibrant crystal pulsated to a gorgeous and golden flaming yellow Diamond, and the oriental Allestra-Terra emerged before them. The artistry and pure perfection of her features revealed the innocence and humility in her loving eyes and face. Her deep midnight tresses were softly held back with 3 headbands; one of icy green jade, one of pure gold, and one of Rose Quartz, as her shining black hair fell to just below her waist. In her hands, she held four heavenly rose buds; one of red, first in beauty but yet humility and perfection; yellow for obedience and discipline; pink for wisdom and grace, and the white rose for innocence and purity. These attributes mirrored the diversified cultures of the very ancient Yellow race that encompassed China and all of her sisters to the north and south, as well as the strand of Pearls in the Pacific beginning with Japan, Hawaii, Samoa, and Tahiti, all families unto God's Yellow Race. They stood mesmerized by Allestra of the Yellow Race as she approached Lynn and placed the perfect white rose bud in Lynn's hands.

"This is the rose bud of perfection and innocence as your unborn child."

"It will be the first seed in Earth's new garden of renewed life that you will plant for all of Humanity".

She then filtered back joining Allestra-Terra, as the great Archangel again spoke.

"Mankind is truly now complete".

"I have always been as one within myself representing the races of the colors within, but you were the ones that had lost one of your fold of Humanity, and now that you have found the lost yellow one, you have finally attained true harmony as one family of God, which is what He had always intended from the beginning of creation". "This is the one true power with which to fight Satan, as he has driven a wedge of hate between the colors to keep them apart with feelings of prejudice, jealousy, and hatred". She continued speaking as she moved toward Felicia, Joe, and Sara.

"God wishes that all races would emulate how your families treat each other, for all of you have treated each other with respect, honor, and love". "You have helped each other, laughed together, cried together, prayed together, and have given your children wisdom and hope".

As the three of them looked at the Archangel, total love and admiration reflected in their eyes at hearing Allestra's words. Allestra then moved freely among them.

"I have called all of you together to explain more about the battle that is very soon approaching". "When God separated a portion of his Holy Waters, he placed them in a large deep cavern below the earth's surface and then covered the ground over with the Great Lake that sits beside you. God favored this lake because although she may be the shallowest of all five, her waters are the most treacherous and she has kept her great secret since the beginning of Creation, for her waters at one time covered all that is now your city". "But over time, and now that the earth has been severely damaged, the lake recedes even further from her shores, leaving a portion of the Holy Waters resting beneath the grounds of this holy cavern". "I have kept watch over the Waters since the beginning of their creation as God has honored me, but now as a portion of them have been less protected by the Lake, I have had to guard them even more closely, for Satan was present as Lucifer the Archangel, when God originally created and hid them beneath the Lake". "Since the earth now needs to be replenished and saved, Satan comes to steal them, but he does not have the power to draw the waters out from their hiding place". "Thus, we do battle, and if he defeats me, he will gain control over the Holy Waters, the earth, and all of humanity". "Therefore, be prepared for what you will see and hear, for when I meet him in battle, he will have his first band of Archangels who were cast out of Heaven with him". "Just as I represent humanity, they represent the full power of his evil, for they are part of him as you are part of me". "You and all those present will see the hideous face of evil and will tremble in terror at the true site of him". "If you believe in God, in the light, in truth, and in Humanity, he will be defeated." Byron suddenly asked,..

"Allestra, How and when will we know what to do?"

Allestra answered him by saying,

"Do not worry Byron, for the spirit of your mind and soul will answer your question when the time comes." Allestra then whispered to Aquila, the Great Eagle, as she walked toward Sam and lifted the great bird off of her shoulder.

"Of all the colors, the Red Race has always revered and protected all that God has created."

"Sam, Son of the Red Race, The Great Eagle honors you for you understand his ways and he will rest upon your shoulder until he is ready to strike at the Raven's stream of darkness."

With these words spoken, the Great Eagle flapped its magnificent wings as Allestra placed Aquila's mighty body onto Sam's shoulder. Billy's face lit up at the site of the mighty Eagle perched upon his very own Son's Shoulder and they were all astounded as they watched and listened intently to Allestra. Allestra then moved very close to Angella and Bent down before her.

"Angella, so pure of heart, you have been chosen to Watch over my Staff while I do battle."

Angella's eyes grew large with unexpected excitement as Allestra handed her the heavenly Staff, but yet the little girl was somewhat afraid that she may not be able to live up to Allestra's expectations and was not worthy enough to be so honored. Before Angella could speak, Allestra answered her

"Do not worry, beloved one; for Byron, Sam, and many others shall be ready to help you when the time comes."

Allestra looked at Byron and at the rest of them as she warned them

"Keep watch over Lynn and Angella, for the Beast is Devious."

Father Vincent's heart raced in terror at the sound of these words.

"Great Warrior of God, he said, "I truly believe in God, but there are times when I doubt myself and I wonder that even though I am a Priest, Am I a coward because I fear what Satan can do?."

"No Vincent", she said. "

Satan should be feared for he is evil, but God is all powerful and almighty and He will not allow this evil to harm any more of his good people." "Before you prepare to leave, there is one more thing I must tell you." "Listen closely to the words I will speak in the mind, for Satan is very shrewd and he still carries with him much power he once had as an Archangel, and he can read the mind and soul as I can, but he has a secret flaw."

"If the soul is pure and clean, the light blinds him and he cannot stay long enough to fully read it, for a clean soul is unbearable to him".

Billy was enthralled and marveled at the site of Allestra, just as he had been from the time he had first seen her broken statue standing on the altar, and in his Apache mind he knew he had been deeply honored, for he was the very first one she had really spoken to when his eyes moved to gaze upon her face that special day in the Church, compelling him to solve her great mystery. As his thoughts flashed back to that moment, Allestra again spoke as she approached Billy.

"During the battle, there is One of you that I will mentally speak to above all others."

Particles of gem-dust swirled around Billy as Allestra locked her angelic eyes on him and spoke to him only with her mind, as the group intensely watched.

"Billy, When the time comes, you moe than anyone will hear my words in your mind, for as I stood beffore you on God's alter, you spoke to me with your mind and soul, and I knew that God had chosen you because of your great faith, for no matter what I speak from my mouth, the others must listen to the words that I will put within your mind."

As Billy gazed into her glorious amethyst eyes, he answered her within his mind,

"Warrior of God, I have hoped and prayed for this moment and I will listen and obey to do all that you ask of me."

Not a sound was heard as they watched in reverence, for they knew that Billy had a special bond with Allestra. The silence was then broken as Allestra told them the most important thing is that

"Don't let your eyes deceive you, for no matter what you think is happening, you must hve faith and obey the words of the chosen one". "The time has come for you to leave me now, for tomorrow is a new beginning for mankind."

As Allestra began to walk back into God's light of warmth and love; reluctantly, the group began to walk back through the Cavern when Chief suddenly turned his head to look at Allestra as he barked and ran toward her one last time, not wanting to leave her. They watched as Allestra stopped to turn around and see Chief approach her. Her compassionate and loving eyes smiled at Chief as she ran her golden hand tenderly over his noble head and elegantly pointed ears, speaking to him in a soothing tone as he nudged her gently, and then affectionately licked her hand; thanking her for his life.

"Loyal and Courageous Creature, I would never forget you or hurt your feelings".

"From the beginning, you have known what you were called to do, and now you have new life that cannot be taken away by evil; so protect your friends as always and do not worry about me, Apollo of Dogs; for God will protect us and Satan will be defeated".

"You must leave me now, Chief, for the time is at hand and you must help me by guarding them."

Chief looked at Allestra with his large, doe-brown eyes and uttered a compliant bark, acknowledging he understood as he ran back to Sam. Tears trickled down Angella's face as she looked back at Allestra and grasped the Royal Staff close to her body, vowing to keep it safe for her dear Archangel.

"Angella," Felicia said quietly, "Come now, you know we must listen to Allestra and leave, for she needs to prepare herself". "I know how you feel, sweetheart, because I feel the same way; but we have to be strong and truly believe that Good will always triumph over evil". "We must have faith, remember?."

Angella looked into her Grandmother's loving eyes as she slowly nodded her head.

"Yes, Grandmama".

"Grandma?, I'm so lucky to have you".

"Please don't ever leave me."

Felicia gently hugged Angella and as the small group of humanity walked back through the Cavern, Sara raised her voice in a sweet song of praise to God's Holy Archangel.

CHAPTER 5

Father Vincent opened the closet and looked at the colored vestments before him. His clean work clothes were torn and ragged after years of use, and Vincent shook his head wondering what he would wear under the Alb. Mark, one of his altar boys saw the look on Vincent's face

"Father Vincent, you know the Alb is long and flows well beneath your knees; surely you can wear it right over your work clothes as you've done in the past".

"It'll be okay, Father Vincent", and as Mark spoke, he winked saying

"and besides you needn't worry about your Roman collar; we all know you're a priest."

Vincent chuckled softly and patted Mark on the shoulder.

"I guess I really don't have a choice Mark, do I'?

"Well my boy, which color shall I choose?"

"You haven't worn the white one in a very long time, Father", Mark replied.

Vincent agreed

"Yes, this is the perfect time to wear the White Alb, for it signifies Purity;

"Yes, Mark, A very good choice indeed".

Mark then helped Father Vincent prepare himself hoping that Troy would soon arrive. Aquila sat upon Sam's shoulder and as they entered the Church, the Great Eagle swiftly soared upward and perched himself on a rafter. Billy refused to be lifted into the pew, as he felt safe and comfortable in the confines of his wheelchair, and so Sara and the others filed into the first row and seated themselves. Sam and Chief were the last to enter, as Billy stayed seated at the outer edge of the pew under Chief's protection. From the rafter above, the Great Eagle sat motionless surveying God's House, ever watchful of Sam, waiting regally for his command. Before Joe took his seat next to Sara, he told her

"I have to see Father Vincent for a few minutes and then I'll be right back."

As Joe entered the Sacristy adjacent to the altar, a young teenage boy rushed by him

"Father Vincent, I'm sorry I'm late, but I had a hard time getting through the crowd to get here."

"That's quite alright, Troy, we still have plenty of time to get ready."

Mark handed Troy his robes, as Troy began to wash his hands and prepare to help serve at the Mass with Mark. Joe then spoke up

"Father Vincent, I just wanted to let you know that everything is ready".

"I've mounted several loud speakers on the roof of the Church so that everyone outside can hear the Mass".

"There are so many people on the Grounds of the Cathedral, that there just isn't enough room for all of them, so I told them that those who couldn't get into the Church would still be able to hear the Mass, and we'll notify them over the loud speakers when the meals are ready to be served."

"Thanks Joe, I truly appreciate everything you and your family have done around here, and I honestly don't know what I would have done without you."

Joe hesitated for a moment and then asked

"Father Vincent, Are you as nervous as I am right now.?"

Vincent touched Joe's hand

"I'm really trying not to be, but we're only human, however, we must have Faith and everything will be as God has promised."

"Yes, Father, I guess I just needed to hear you say that to help me feel a little better."

"Well Father, Sara's saving a seat for me, so I guess I'll see you at Mass", Joe said smiling.

Father Vincent returned the smile as Joe left the Sacristy and took his place next to Sara. The three youths pushed their way through the crowd as they made their way on the grounds of the Cathedral.

"Come on Frankie, You don't really believe this bull story about some stupid battle, do ya.?", said one of the boys.

"Yeah, I don't see why we have to go in there when all we want is the free meal anyway, but I wish there really was a battle so we could join in on the fun", said the other boy as the two of them laughed.

Frankie looked at them, shaking his head in disgust,

"Look, I'm going in there whether you want to or not, and besides, I've done a lot of thinking lately, and you know what?" "I don't think I want you guys as friends anymore."

The two boys frowned and visibly looked agitated as they replied,

"Okay Frankie, if that's the way you want it, that's what you'll get, but we're warning you; nobody walks away from us and when your day in church is over, we'll be waiting right here for a real battle, if you know what we mean"?

Frankie turned his back on them as he entered the Cathedral alone in hopes of getting a seat. The Church was quickly filling up as Rabbi Silverman and his family took their seats directly behind Felicia and the others. Soon after, Father's Thomas and Bennett entered with their families and sat directly across the main aisle from Rabbi Silverman. Frankie walked down a side aisle looking for a seat and as he approached the front of the Church, he saw there was room for one more in the pew behind Sam and Billy. On entering the pew, he accidentally bumped into the back of Sam's head; and as Sam turned around, he recognized Frankie as one of the boys who had attacked him on his way home from the Great Hall. Frankie felt awkward and was embarrassed about the fact that he had tried to steal from Sam, but he also felt the need to apologize

"Hi, I don't know your name, but I'm Frank, and I'm sorry about what happened that day. "Would you accept my apology?".

With that being said, Frank extended his hand in friendship. Sam hesitated slightly, but then shook Frank's hand and warmly accepted his apology as he smiled

"I'm Sam."

Byron could hear what was being said as he tilted his head over his shoulder to look behind him, and with one eyebrow raised in triumph, Byron nodded his head in approval, affirming that it was about time Frankie finally did something right for a change.

Frankie gratefully shook Sam's hand

"Thanks",

as he beamed broadly and took his seat in the pew behind them. By this time, the Church was full of families of all races and creed, old and young alike, with some standing in the back of the Church and others in the aisles as they gathered together in prayer and waited for the service to begin. As Father Vincent and his two altar boys ascended the altar, Angella inched closer to her grandmother, while tightly clutching Allestra's Holy staff that ran across her thighs and onto Byron's lap. After the first scriptural reading, Father Vincent then proceeded to read the Gospel from God's Holy Book to the people. When he was done, he moved to the pulpit where he began his sermon by telling everyone that all races should honor each other as God created them equally in heart, mind, and soul. Father Vincent spoke about having Faith in the belief that God would restore the earth in all of her glorious nature, and upon hearing these words, Satan could hardly contain himself as he hid within the sanctity of God's Holy House. He despised being forced to listen to these repugnant and meaningless human words, but until the time was right for him to strike, he told himself that he must endure this pain only a little while longer. He then smugly sneered to himself with great pride, while he thought how these despicable humans would react to find that he, Satan, was among them in their so-called holy place of worship. Satan then cast his vision over the people searching for a gesture, a smell, or a feeling of where Allestra may be hiding, for he told himself she must be there somewhere among them as he was. As his nostrils flared open, they caught a slight odor of something different, but yet familiar.

"What was this odor", he thought to himself, "for I know I've smelled this before".

Like a crazed bloodhound on the trail, he voraciously followed and quickly stalked the scent over the rows of people as the odor grew stronger and closer. Suddenly his nostrils flared even wider, tracking the scent to the final destination of his prey; and there before him, his gleaning eyes revealed the face and reflection of the "Yellow One". At the site of Lynn, Satan became incensed with rage and wanted nothing better than to vent his violent anger and kill her on the spot, but

"No." "Now is not the time."

So, he controlled himself for he knew somehow Hemortus had betrayed him, and yet

"I searched his soul for a speck of light and there was None to be found."

Satan was sure that Allestra had been the perpetrator and this was only one more humiliation added to his vendetta of revenge against her, but Hemortus still would not go unpunished as he would also feel the pains of this treachery; for Satan now would deviously test Hemortus this day to justify his vindictive torment. Father Vincent returned to the altar for the most sacred part of the Mass in which he prepared the Bread of Life and the Venerated Chalice of Salvation, so that all souls could partake as one with Jesus in remembrance of His Last Supper. As the priest held the sacred Chalice in the air for all to see, Satan thought to himself,

"This is the moment to draw her out into the Open."

The expression on Mark's face was one of absolute horror as he pulled Father Vincent away from the altar while Troy's body changed before everyone's eyes into the ultimate entity from Hell. The great marble floor of the Cathedral cracked and shook as the congregation gasped and screamed in terror at the transformation of Troy into the Supreme Enemy of God and of mankind. When Satan emerged from Troy's false shell of a body, he was simply dressed as a common man wearing black shoes, a pair of worn gray pants and a slightly open shirt revealing his masculine neck line. On each wrist, he wore the once beautiful wrist bands so lovingly presented to him, but were now host to his vileness and corruption, as was his eternal ring of fire that adorned his finger. His thick black hair had a beautiful blue/black luster to it and his skin was smooth and fine, covering the rugged bone structure of a shockingly-handsome face that artfully framed his large, moss-green eyes, with lips that parted sensually as he began to speak. Father Vincent held the Chalice close to his heart guarding it with his life, as he and Mark had inched away from the altar and were now standing at the base of Allestra's statue. Men and women hid their eyes and wept in fear, not wanting to gaze upon the evil from Hell. Satan took a few steps forward and began to speak in a gentle, clear and crystal voice; and as the people heard the sound of his voice, they cautiously raised their eyes not knowing what to expect, but at the site of him they were astounded to see that he did not look as they had perceived him to be.

"Since the beginning of time, you have heard my name and you have heard many things about me, some true and some untrue." "Let me begin by saying that I am Satanus-Legion, Prince and Ruler, most powerful Archbeing who sat beside the OTHER for many eons, and I loved and honored him as you do." "I was but a naive child but as I grew in strength, I became "Legion", and I began to question certain things and because of this and the others' jealousies, I was banished from his side." "I say to you Mankind, Do I look like a Demon?", "Do I sound like a Demon?" "They would have you believe that I am; but I am here to show you that I am none of these things." "I Say to you, What kind of a God lets you starve and die in the streets.?" "What kind of a God gives you no shade or relief?" "What kind of a God lets you suffer from War."? "And, What kind of a God gives you no Water to drink?" "I have come here to do battle for Thy Water so that Mankind may quench their thirst once more." "But, where is this great Warrior, Allestra, that I am to battle?" "Is she a coward or a liar?" "So now then, here is what I offer you to prove myself."

Satan felt immense gratification in his words knowing that to deceive just a few of them would bring sadness to God, and their souls would automatically be his if they betrayed their faith; and so he continued his evil web of deceit and temptation, hoping to draw Allestra out into the open for battle. He drew his wrist bands together and a bountiful table appeared laden with large lush fruits, breads, vegetables, meats, deserts, wine, and fine goblets of gold. He walked toward the table and poured some wine into one of the goblets, and as he took a sip, he could see the hunger and thirst in the eyes of his potential victims.

"Come and eat".

"Drink with me for I offer you all the succulence of the earth for the rest of your lives."

Again, at the touch of his wrist bands, Satan produced all manner of clothing before their very eyes. "Drink with me, for I offer you all the fine linens, woolen, and silk clothing for the rest of your lives." A third time, he drew his wrist bands together and a large golden basket appeared overflowing with

glittering jewels of every size and shape as they poured forth like a river onto the bottom step of the altar. "I offer your hearts all the gems the earth has kept hidden, for the rest of your lives."

Three sacks then appeared, and when he opened these, gold and silver coins along with paper bills of money burst out overlapping the jewels upon the step of the altar.

"Do not be afraid."

"Come and drink with me, for I offer you the riches of life for the rest of your days."

Their eyes grew larger in disbelief looking at the riches being offered to them as Satan continued to speak.

"There is one thing missing that I do not have to offer you, for I must gain control of the Water that your God has denied you, while you die of thirst; and once this is accomplished, You will never thirst as long as you shall live." "All of this I promise without asking anything in return."

He motioned to the people with outstretched arms, beckoning them to come upon the altar and partake with him, without obligation. Some were apprehensive as they looked around at each other not knowing what to do, not knowing if they should believe him, but he was so handsome and sincere in his words that they wanted to believe in him, for he looked and sounded like one of them. Besides, what harm could there be, as they had gone without so very much for such a long time, that they felt they deserved to share in the abundance before them. The two youths had broken through the crowd and entered the Church, and seeing all that was offered, were among the first to accept Satan's gifts, as they were the first to drink from the golden goblets. Frankie yelled out to them in vain, but they were already upon the altar enjoying the bounty as were others also who willingly accepted Satan's gifts of deceit and greed. Father Vincent was stunned in disbelief and could hardly speak, as Rabbi Silverman stood and shouted to the people on the altar.

"You are like the evil idolaters who carved the Golden Calf and then worshiped it; and God will punish you for this as he punished them."

Rabbi Silverman's words gave Father Vincent the courage to speak as he pleaded to the people accepting Satan's offerings.

"Children of God, Stop and Think that you are betraying the Almighty One and your very souls. Don't accept his evil gifts. "Please, Go Back before it's too late."

But it was too late, for Satan stood there with a glint in his eye and a smile on his lips as he spoke to the priest.

"Priest, What does your Goblet have to offer them?, for yours is empty while mine is Full",

as he raised his Goblet of Wine in defiance and triumph to his lips. Felicia, Angella, and the rest of the people, never imagined that something like this would happen, and they sat wondering where Allestra was and why she wasn't there defending them, but they kept remembering and telling themselves to have Faith. Satan thought to himself,

"All of this I have done, and she still hides herself", and he knew that he must get down to the real business at hand, for he only had one hour within the Circle of Eternal Life. He knew he must soon pierce the Circle of Eternal Life to gain him more time, as he thought about his plan to force Allestra out into the open, face to face in battle. The people on the altar were oblivious to everything or anyone around them, enjoying all that Satan had provided, for he had cast a spell on them closing their eyes, ears, and hearts; so therefore, they did not hear or see the screams of the people or the demons entering the Church. In the distance, screams and pleas to God could be heard from the people gathered on the grounds outside, and their terror-filled voices grew louder as the heavy Baroque doors of the Cathedral broke open flying off of their steel hinges, as Kartos and Arachnon entered God's House striking complete fear into the congregation's heart and soul. As they led the way, Hemortus followed behind them carrying Satan's Spear of Gold and Silver, while Ravanu and Saddesma brought up the rear. Men and women cowered in horror trying to somehow hide within their pews while shielding their children and babies, for they were aghast at the site of Satan's four generals before them.

Although trembling with fear, Father Vincent, yelled to the people,

"You must have faith and believe".

The four unholy warriors proceeded to walk up the main aisle of the Cathedral with Hemortus in the middle, slowly looking out of the corner of his eyes hoping for a glimpse of Allestra. Each of their ankles revealed a 1-inch high, gray colored small wing, which were now only faded remnants of what they once symbolized. The four demons were almost alike for each was at least 7 feet tall, with talons for nails hideously deformed and arched downward, scraping the marble floor as they advanced. Their feet were bound in sandals with straps that cris-crossed around their ankles and stopped at mid-calf. Three, 2-inch long silver chains dangled from the top strap at each outer leg, clanging to their cadence as they advanced up the aisle toward the steps of the altar. Their faces were partially covered with plates of tarnished and blackened silver that covered their forehead, the bridge and plane of their nose and chin, exposing their flared nostrils in defiance and thin lips of charcoal gray, with scars of sin on either cheek of their face. Their massive bowed chests were bare except for two thick black straps that cris-crossed their torso. Each wore the headdress of Caligula entering into war with a black Roman plume that crowned the top of their loathsome battle regalia. The flesh on their exposed arms, legs, and hands was dry and ashen, with a few open sores secreting their foul odor from Hell, as they commandingly marched up the cracked, marble aisle, relishing each step taken in God's House. While advancing, they simultaneously lunged their long spears at the people, and the glare of haunting hatred in their eyes cast out sporadic bursts of black and gray rays, forcing the people to cringe and cower in submission at the site of their evil power. Hemortus was dressed in rags of blood-dried cloth, but his flesh was as theirs, and his eyes were almost lifeless as he slowly followed them toward the altar. Father Vincent held the Sacred Chalice even closer to his heart as everyone froze in terror at the evil approaching. Angella shut her eyes, clutching the Royal Staff ever so tightly, as all of them within the pew held on to each other, praying this nightmare would end, while Chief growled in an intense low tone waiting impatiently for the Great Master's command to attack. Kartos and Arachnon stopped before the first step that led to God's Holy Altar while Hemortus stood waiting beside the first pew, and as Hemortus stood there, he heard the familiar sound of the Dog beast growl. Afraid to turn his head, he carefully moved his eyes hoping to catch a glimpse of something familiar and from the outer edge of his right eye, Byron came into view; one of the frail humans that he so longed to be like again; and although he didn't have a heart or soul, Hemortus could feel something beat within him for he knew the Great Angel must surely be close by, and his soul was in agony as he dared to hope that maybe he could pass the test. At the site of his Generals, Satan's figure rose to a height of nearly 8 feet tall. His feet were now bound in black Roman sandals with straps that cris-crossed up around his ankles and rose to below his knee caps. His powerful, smoothly-muscled, yet lithe body was clothed in strips of black, supple leather signifying the uniform of Caligula, Rome's imperial emperor who was noted for his insatiable appetite for murder, torture, and reprehensible debauchery that could never be quenched. Resting in the middle of his silver breastplate was a 20 carat dark purple Amethyst, subtly smoldering as if telling the world that it alone held Satan's hidden secrets embedded deep within its soul. His black Cloak was draped and fastened at each shoulder with a diamond; each partially filled with red carbons of death producing piercing red embers borne of the River Carnage, as the Roman cloak flowed to his ankles. His forehead was adorned with three headbands; two of black gold and one of red, bracing his thick and healthy black hair that framed his handsome face. Silence and the fear of death came over the people as Kartos bowed first to Satan and then raised his hellish, low pitched voice

"Priest of the OTHER, I am Kartos, General to Satan, first in Battle by his side".

"As I have bowed down to him so will mankind honor him for he is Supreme Prince of the core within, and unto all universal levels below and within the mighty inferno."

Sam hoped and prayed that Allestra would soon come to their rescue, and in his mind Billy answered him.

"Do not lose faith my son, for she is here among us, waiting for the right moment."

Saddesma then spoke in a higher pitched male/female voice

"I am Saddesma, 3rd Power in the temple of Satanus, Liaison and Queen to his flames of desire". Saddesma moved closer to the railing that led to the altar and jerked her head toward Father Vincent and Mark.

"Vincent, Will Thee not Share thy Cup with Me.?"

The look of horror on Father Vincent's face could not be mistaken as he thought out loud

"How Dare you think that I will let you put your filthy corrupt hands or lips on the Savior's Holy Chalice?"

Saddesma then laughed as though she had a great secret horror about to be fulfilled.

"Priest of Rome, You deny to share with me, but yet you have shared your cup with others of different beliefs?"

With a smirk on her face, Saddesma flicked her gray tongue over her lips and gazed toward Angella.

"Surely, You would not deny Myself and sweet, innocent Angella to share a drink of blood from thy Cup?" At the sound of Angella's name, Felicia screamed in horror as Saddesma willfully moved toward the first pew and Angella. Angella hid her head behind Felicia's back desperately holding on to her Grandmother; and as Saddesma approached the pew, she bent her head and arm over the railing sneering in delight and relishing the thought of touching the pure and innocent child. Felicia bravely stood up, trying to shield Angella with her body and screamed

"You sacrilegious bitch, you keep away from her because I'll fight and die first, before I ever let you touch and corrupt her."

Chief's growls were becoming louder and meaner as he jumped over the pew ready to attack. As Saddesma hideously laughed and reached out to grab Angella, both Chief & Byron lunged at her at the same time. Chief was up on his hind legs and his height was as tall as the demon, as he viciously tore into the back of her neck while Byron slashed at her hand with his knife. No blood could be seen as the knife cut into her lifeless and ashen skin which only purpose was to hide the rotten meat within. Saddesma felt nothing but anger at what this human dared to do, as the other unholy angels of darkness looked-on

and anxiously waited for Satan's command to join the attack. Saddesma threw Chief off of her back and he landed at least 8 feet away, but she knew the Dog Beast would again attack, for he was protected and could not die. Saddesma's voice changed to the evil viscousness that she represented, and she turned on Byron ready to destroy him before Chief could regain his balance. No human had ever attacked her and she wanted to punish him, as she gained her momentum in offense and moved toward him in a murderous rage. Striking with inhuman swiftness, she grabbed Byron by the neck and raised him off the ground holding him in the air as everyone screamed in terror.

"I'm going to bite your head off like a Chicken, but before I do, I think I'll have some fun with you and peel your skin first."

Jus as Saddesma jerked Byron closer to her, a rumbling sound was heard and felt, getting louder and stronger as the whole Cathedral shook from its very foundation to its mighty arched ceiling while it's light fixtures swayed back and forth. The Great Eagle held on to his perch with his powerful talons and balanced himself with his lofty wings as the congregation wept and prayed aloud for God to Save them. Saddesma reluctantly dropped Byron to the floor, as Satan quickly commanded his 4 generals and Hemortus to stand beside him on God's altar. Satan stood his ground, for he knew it was Allestra-Terra and he was on the threshold of his long-awaited moment of power and revenge. Father Vincent hung on to the base of Allestra's statue for he would not abandon God's altar, and as he turned to tell Mark to run for safety, Vincent's heart was in awe as were the rest of them, at what was transpiring before them and Vincent thought.

"It was never really Mark at all; it was Allestra-Terra all along who had helped him in the sacristy and stood beside him on the altar."

As her supernatural figure rose to that of Satan's height, the magnificence and power of her presence was seen and felt throughout the Church. Her sandals were bronze with cris-crossed straps that securely protected her rose-colored feet and ankles. She was clothed as a Roman in a slatted skirt of leather strips in white with muted shades of light rose and purplish tones, as the strips of leather started at her waist and fell barely above her knees. A 20 carat stellar shaped Amethyst Crystal of sparkling perfection rested in the center of her Platinum and white Gold-inlaid mesh breastplate, emitting it's brilliant rays of God's perfection and universal power. As she lifted her head in full view, her skin was the color of a glorious rose tone basking in God's illumination that was cast upon her cheeks and ignited the canvas of her flawless features including her profound and magnetic, amethyst eyes, lashes, and lips. One golden pulsating headband framed her forehead and temples as it embraced her variegated and glorious hair. The other two headbands now rested on each of her upper arms and in her hands, she held a pure Platinum staff. The people remained galvanized at the site of the Holy Warrior that God had sent to defend them, and the 4 demons wanted nothing more than to attack her, but Satan lifted his arm against them and silently commanded them to wait. Allestra spoke, but Satan could not bear to look upon her face and so he turned his head and eyes from her. Hoping not to betray himself, Hemortus tried to hide the look of life and hope

in his eyes at the glorious vision before him, and he trembled in fear wondering what the test would be and what he would do. In a stern and commanding voice, Allestra asked

"Who is it that surely treads so closely on the brink of destruction, that he dares to bring his corruption and evil into God's Holy Tabernacle?"

Without looking at Allestra, Satan replied

"It is I, Legion and Ruler of the Inferno's Epicenter and of all dimensions within and below its House; And who art thou to tell me where to tread?"

Satan slowly moved his eyes to catch a glimpse of her as she answered.

"I am the 9th Power who dwells in the 5th House of the Lord who is creator and master of all Universes and of the Eternal Infinity". "My Lord and God calls me Allestra-Terra, Archangel and Protector of the Waters of Creation, Warrior of God in his Heaven, and guardian of the colors of Mankind." "Shall I tell them why Lucifer is afraid to look upon my face?" "Does it remind him of the truth and of what he once was?"

Satan now moved his head and eyes in her direction, staring at her majestic presence, for the color of her skin reminded him of what he once reflected and she mirrored the beauty he had once called his own. He did not want to hear the name that God had bestowed upon him coming from her lips, for it forced him to remember that he was the first and only Archangel ever created with a satin rose skin tone that rivaled the special flower in God's heavenly Garden; and as he continued gazing at her, memories and mixed feelings flashed through his mind for he was there when God created her. She was the fifth of all Archangels to be created, and at first he loved her for she was the closest in beauty to him, but later he had become angry and jealous because he was no longer the only Rose in the Garden.

"He had no right, for I did all that he asked of me",
said Satan raising his voice.
"Lucifer, do you not remember"? continued Allestra.
"I was his first and he betrayed me, for he gave you the privilege of protecting the Waters, but it was I who walked beside him at the dawn of creation, and it should have been I who was so honored."

Allestra then interrupted him.

"Lucifer, it is true; you were God's first and most beautiful and favored Archangel ever created, and he gave you awesome power above all that came after you; but this was not enough for you."
"You were with him from the beginning as he created the Earth, the sun, the moon, and the stars". He honored you and gave you ultimate power to control and protect the Moon, the stars, and the light.", But again, this was not enough."

As She spoke, Satan looked away from her again, for the pain of her words stung his dark soul.

"As he created more of us, you became increasingly jealous and you slowly corrupted and gathered an army against your Creator."

"Still, our Father would have forgiven you, but then you did the unthinkable when you tempted his creation of mankind into sin, for they were not as strong as we."

Satan slowly began to seethe with jealousy as he looked upon Allestra's face.

"Yes, Yes, I tempted them, and do you know why?"

"Because he loved those weak willed mortals more than he loved us."

"He lived for them and not for us, doting over his frail new creation while he forgot about us, and I wanted him to feel the pain as he made us feel."

Allestra then forcefully spoke out against Satan.

"The darkness within your soul masks the light of truth, for Dominus did not hurt us".

"It is within your mind only that you were the one who felt unjustifiably hurt, for your hatred and jealousy has scarred your thoughts within your unholy soul." "Since we were created as the most powerful supernatural beings that infinity has ever know, God wanted us to teach, nurture, and guide Humanity". "Therefore, He was going to honor you by putting you in Command of his plan, for Mankind was but a child and vulnerable in his new life, but you used your great power against them, twisted his thinking, and then led them into sin." "Look what your evil has done to you, for your eyes mirror the sins of your soul." "Once, your eyes sparkled with God's eternal life and were more brilliant than any of ours, but you were blinded by jealousy and hatred just as you felt when He created me.", said Allestra.

Visibly shaken by her words, Satan turned toward Allestra and tried to control himself as he spoke "No, Allestra."

"From the moment you were created I loved you, for you were the only other created as I, a beautiful and glorious Rose, and I wanted to be with you always." "Allestra, you can still be a great leader by my side, and I will forgive thee for turning against me." "If you join with me, our power will be truly unmatched even by HIM, and we can rule all of Heaven and Earth together." "Give my thy water and Denounce him, and we will rule together for eternity, for You will have all that you desire."

But, Allestra's loyalty was to God.

"Lucifer, there is nothing that you can offer to make me betray the Creator, for my loyalty and honor is to my father who loves his children, and that is all I desire."

Satan's voice wreaked with agitation

"Would a God who loved thee, let you waste unhonored centuries of time guarding a dust bowl of a cavern.?" "I offer thee the keys of my kingdom and the kingdom of creation. Together, we can gather millions of souls which will give us unlimited power to rule all of Creation; And finally, My Allestra-Terra, I offer thee myself".

With each response from Allestra, Satan's expression grew more vile and angry.

"There is but one key and one creator, and my allegiance is to Him, for he is the Key to all life". "There is no power greater than what God has already given me, for he is the great master of the Universe and beyond.", "And, it is you that should cry out for forgiveness from the Lord for all evil that you have done and brought upon his children." "Yes, I joined in battle against thee in God's House, and I do so again, Lucifer, for thou art corrupt, unholy, and have betrayed all that God has created."

Lucifer's piercing eyes mirrored his angry and hate filled soul as he commanded Hemortus to bring him his sword. As Lucifer grasped his sword, he glared into Hemortus' eyes silently telling him that he knew of his betrayal. Hemortus desperately tried to hide the terror he felt within himself, not wanting to think about what Lucifer would do to him. The Church quaked as Ravanu moved closer to Satan and conjured up 6 large Ravens, awaiting his command. Satan rubbed his Ring of Fire and the people trembled in fear as they watched him point his silver sword downward drawing out the Black Venom of Darkness from the very bowels of Hell. The hideous unearthly creature was 3 feet long, slender, and coal black with small but thin, translucent red fins on either side of its head, its middle, and at its tail. Lynn gasped in terror as she touched her belly protecting her unborn child and desperately clung to Byron.

No longer able to control himself, Satan's voice wreaked of hatred and contempt.

"Allestra, the battle begins and I will pierce thy Circle, for now the time has come for thee to pay for thy crimes against me." "I shall enjoy destroying thy soul to gain thy Waters, and then I will devour Gabriel and Michael and the rest of thy Legion who cast me out."

The Great Bald Eagle instinctively knew that the moment had arrived, and the Mighty Eagle crouched his majestic head, focusing his keen site on the enemies below and anticipating Sam's mental command. The 6 ravens took hold of the snake's fins with their feet and they rose in flight, carrying their destructive cargo as they flew through the opening of a large partially-broken church window. Sam looked up at "Aquila" the Great Eagle and spoke within it's mind.

"Soar Swiftly My Friend; Protect the Circle and Destroy the Creator's enemies."

With a bolt of lightening speed, Aquila powerfully flew across the width and height of the Church, and as he approached the stained glass window, he placed his wings at his side and dove directly through the window, breaking and crushing the rest of it, and sending more chunks of colored glass to the ground, as he then arched his wings outward and quickly flew after his prey. As Aquila flew through the window, Satan looked toward Allestra and now became incensed with rage and fury at the site of her, for he could no longer contain his animosity and jealously. Lucifer pointed his mighty sword toward the floor and it seemed as though the light of day paled as the candles in the Church flickered and wavered in a cold and unholy breeze that enveloped them. The people whimpered in fear begging for God's forgiveness while gray and silver lightening-rods emanated from the tip of the sword and crackled in all directions. A shroud of unholy mist slowly seeped in and around the Cathedral while its mighty rafters and beams squeaked and moaned under the stress of being caught in the clutches of a mighty earthquake. Cracks in the marble floor broke open as the walls of the Church split their seams and crumbled on to the outside grounds of the Cathedral, crushing and trapping the people outside. Many of the people inside and outside of the Cathedral were thrown about as they frantically ran for safety and screamed for mercy. The cavern beneath the Church shook violently as it slowly began to rise up toward the floor of the Great Cathedral. The unholy breeze became a Satanic whirlwind of destruction unhinging rows of pews and throwing the terrified people deeper into the black nightmare of Lucifer's unleashed fury and anger. His ungodly voice pierced the air as he called upon the cavern below and its hidden secret to rise in his name with all of the supernatural powers within him. Great squares of marble and church pews were pushed upward while simultaneously, masses of debris fell downward into the cavern as it raised upward and through the buckling floor of the Cathedral. The nonbelievers on the altar who had fallen prey to Satan's temptation were now brought back to reality, begging for help and screaming in fear as huge beams from the Church's lofty ceiling crushed their mortal bodies. The inferno opened widely with unparalleled gravity pulling it's helpless prey through the burning gates of hell, incarcerating the unwilling souls for Satan's eternal pleasure. Portions of the congregation wept openly as they clung to pews, fallen statues, and remnants of walls, while large pieces of stalagmite formations within the cavern steadily rose upward.

 His enemies were well within his site and Aquila instinctively knew that he must swiftly attack before the reptile's fins grew into giant wings; for then he would never be able to overtake and kill it. With all of his power and speed, Aquila flew into the heavens circling above the Ravens. In one fell swoop, he began his quickened descent through the clouds and attacked the first two ravens that were at the head of the sleeping reptile. As he killed one raven, the other broke off to turn and fight, but he would be no match for the Great Eagle, as Aquila pierced it's heart with his beak. The other two Ravens that were holding up the midsection of the reptile, flew forward to the Reptile's head to replace the front position, as the other Ravens steadfastly brought up the tail. Again, Aquila flew above the clouds and as he began to descend upon his prey, his sharp vision could see the evil reptile's wings already beginning to grow so that it might soon fly on its own. With even swifter speed, the Bald Eagle, swooped and again attacked the Ravens at the front of the snake-like creature, ripping into their hearts. As the dead ravens' bodies spiraled toward the earth, the other two could no longer hold up the reptile's tail, for it had already become larger and it's weight was now too great for them to carry alone. The remaining two ravens let go of the snake's tail and retreated to their master's dark realm, as Satan's demon tumbled through the air, falling toward the earth below. Wasting no time, Aquila dove toward the reptile, for he knew he must stop it from reaching the Circle of Eternal Life. As the Great Eagle attacked it, the now Giant Reptile's body stopped in mid-air gaining control of itself, for it's wing span was already 3 times greater than that of Aquila's. The evil reptile raised it's slimy head and opened its spotted eyes relishing the thought of it's first meal. It opened it's mouth sucking the air inward pulling the Great Eagle toward it's poison tongue as Aquila flapped his wings furiously, fighting for his life. Exhausted, the Eagle barely broke away and again bounded for the safety of the high clouds, for the Reptile's skin and large wings were too thin to tolerate the sun and air in the Eagle's Lofty domain. Aquila gathered his strength as he initiated the attack again and headed straight for the Reptile's tail hoping to destroy it's back wings. In one bold dive, the Eagle pierced the back opaque wings of the demon, and then hastened quickly to the safety of the clouds, to again regain his strength and rest for his final attack on the enemy below. Aquila knew he must hurry for the Creature was still powerful enough to fly, and now the demon was not far from the Circle of Eternal Life. Aquila then climbed higher and higher into the heavens, reaching his ultimate altitude above the clouds, for this would be his most important and final assault on the evil creature. The mighty eagle shrieked his call to the Great Creator one last time as he broke through the clouds diving straight for the midsection of wings on his enemy, hoping to completely destroy him. The Great Eagle dove with unequaled power and speed toward the Reptile's mid-section, and as Aquila came closer, the beast borne of evil stopped in mid-air and balanced its body upright, whipping the air with its blood-colored wings from Hell. Again, it opened its mouth sucking the air inward and trapping the eagle in a whirlpool of wind, as the monster pulled the courageous eagle toward him like a magnet. Aquila desperately flapped his wings as the repugnant demon drew the eagle closer to his poisonous tongue and mouth. By this time, Aquila was near total exhaustion, but still valiantly continued to fight for his survival and that of mankind. As Satan's demon thrust out his tongue to snare his captive, the waxen flask around Aquila's neck, bounced and swung through the air like a small pendulum. Through the slashed opening in the flask, one precious drop of the Holy Waters slowly tumbled through the air and squarely landed on the tongue of Lucifer's snake sending shock waves through its hideous form. The Reptile of darkness shrieked and jolted in pain as rays of light and electricity ignited arcs of magnetic-colored and crystallized-bolts through the reptile's convulsing body and wings, disintegrating it from the face of God. Aquila regained his strength and flew above the clouds once more as he majestically soared onward to the Circle of Eternal Life where he perched himself at the very pinnacle of a sheath. The Magnificent Eagle then cried out to God in thanks and simultaneously flapped his thunderous wings in celebration, as this was the custom of his ancestors in telling nature of his victory; for at last, he alone was the rightful and lofty guardian of God's Eternal Circle.

CHAPTER 6

Not even the strong rays of the sun star could penetrate the supernatural black clouds of darkness that shrouded the Crystal Cavern. The altar, which was all that was left of the Great Cathedral, now crookedly stood at the Cavern's center. Within the dark clouds of gray and black, small specs of debris and dirt floated through the mass of thick air, as only moans of pain and grief were heard. A few bent and mis-shapen candles undyingly wavered and flickered through the seeds of darkness, barely casting their shadows on the glorious crystal icicles, as Lucifer hid within the blackness of his soul. Joe pulled Sara from beneath one of the pews, as she winced in pain from bruises and cuts on her leg. Felicia comforted Sara as she tried to clean up some of the cuts on Sara's leg, while Sam and Byron checked the rest of the group to see if everyone else was alright. Rabbi Silverman and his family also joined with them as they all huddled together in one corner of the cavern near several overturned pews, cringing in fear and praying for Allestra. Out of breath, Frankie crawled over to Sam and Byron and told them that most of the people seemed to be okay and many of them were in small groups hiding throughout the great Cavern. Sam looked over at his father and saw that one of the wheels on Billy's wheel chair was stuck in a crevice and could not move. As Frankie helped Sam free the wheelchair and pull Billy to safety, Chief instinctively began pacing and circling the group, pushing his massive body up against Angella and the others, coercing them to move further behind the safety of the pews. As they huddled together, Angella hid Allestra's staff between two of the overturned pews in front of her. She and Lynn clung to each other within the protection of Felicia, Billy, and the others by their sides. Chief then jumped over the pews and sniffed the air to make sure that everyone was accounted for and none were lost; and only then, did he take his place beside Sam. Sam could feel nothing but sheer adrenalin surge through his body and with a lump in his throat, he looked at Byron who was also experiencing the same feeling that was about to become the most monumental moment of their lives. Father Vincent and Rabbi Silverman prayed for Allestra-Terra to once again prevail against the evil presence and banish him from the earth, as he had been banished from God's heavenly house since the birth of man. The four Archangels of mankind muted together becoming one, and as the entity rose to a height of 8 feet tall, God's Mighty Archangel stood upon the altar, as she was now transformed into the powerful Warrior of God that no human eyes had ever beheld. From head to foot, her skin was now the true war color of deep rose as she took her battle stance, striking fear into all evil hearts. Her feet were bare and a band of pure platinum, given up by the earth at the first dawn of time, hugged each ankle. A one-inch tall, small feathered, white wing protruded slightly outward and upward, just above each ankle bone. Starting at mid-thigh, pointed bands of platinum dust cris-crossed her deep glowing, rose-colored body, as the platinum dust intertwined across her bodice and faded from view behind her neck. Allestra's forearms were bound in her familiar wrist bands of the Holy gems of the earth, and her shoulders and arms were bare except for gold and platinum bands that wrapped each upper arm in spiritual power. Braided and weaved with strands of platinum, her hair was the color of muted champagne with a hint of rose perfection, as the platinum emitted soft sparks of heavenly sheen and luster. A series of three, graduated, v-shaped bands of the same pure ore graced her forehead and ended at the bridge of her nose. As Allestra-Terra raised the platinum staff of war above her head, her piercing amethyst eyes surveyed the cavern, searching for the evil presence that she knew was lurking on holy ground. In the open, but yet hidden in darkness, Satan's horrific eyes glared of hatred and revenge as he grabbed Hemortis by the neck and whispered..........

"When the time comes, you will obey my command for no matter what thy sweet Allestra has promised thee, your fate was sealed long ago and your captive soul remains as mine, eternally unworthy to see the grace of light in the OTHER's eyes".

Powerless, Hemortus listened in complete fear and sorrow as Satan threatened him.

"Heed my words, slave of sin, and do not betray me again; for I will sear thy flesh before I skin it off, and I promise thee that your screams of pain will bring me pleasure through all of Hell's eternity".

Allestra-Terra touched one of her ankle bracelets with the staff of war, as a large platinum circle swirled in the air. A ray of amethyst from her eyes multiplied it into thousands of tiny, searching, purple colored flecks bursting in all directions of the cavern, seeking to highlight the darkness of evil. No longer demure and soft spoken, Allestra's crystal voice rang through the cavern as a Warrior Archangel of God's creation, for now her supernatural vision could see the black vortex of sin as the arrows of truth defined its form. "Enemy of God, the end of the fifth eon has come, and thus we meet in battle again."

Hemortus cringed in fear for he unwillingly stood along-side the black veiled vortex of evil. Their hearts beat anxiously as the terrified people in the cavern watched in silence behind the safety of large boulders, overturned pews, and statues.

"Uncloak thyself, Devil of Deceit, for I command thee in God's Name".

The lifeless shroud of the black vortex twisted and swirled giving way to a charcoal colored mist that also faded, revealing the cloaked figure of Satan and his generals as they stood before Allestra. No longer was his voice sweet for he now spoke with contempt and hatred toward the Great Warrior.

"You have had many chances Allestra."

"No longer shall I ask thee for thy Water."

"The fifth eon has ended and now I shall torture thee and take what is mine".

Hemortus cowered in terror as he quickly scurried to the other side of the pews which separated him from Sam, Byron and the others, for he knew what mankind was about to see. As Satan's four generals filtered into his cloaked body, Allestra-Terra cried out to all of the people.

"Behold the True Nature of Evil".

"Humanity, Look with your eyes and your souls and remember this day; for Behold God's Enemy, Behold My Enemy, and Behold the Ultimate Enemy of Mankind and of all Creation."

"Behold the true Beast that calls himself Legion and Satanus."

His repugnance and vileness was undefinable as well as unspeakable, for he was marked with the horror of his sins equal to nothing ever seen on this earth. His evil permeated the already thick air, for as beautiful and powerful as Allestra was, so he was vile and corrupt with pulsating living scars of sin covering his entire lithe and agile body. The main scar of sin was thick and raised, as it curled in the center and defined the very core of his evil heart and black soul, and sent out trailers on a vine of gray and murky raised scars over his chest and entire body, ending at the toes of his bare feet. He was no longer deceivingly handsome, for now Satan's face projected the true marks of evil, as his face was etched with grotesque pulsating scars of sin that fanned his forehead, outer edges of his eyes, and temples, which then finally furrowed themselves into his coarse and semi-hairless scalp. What the people saw so horrified them that many could hardly scream, for the image of evil before them sent tumultuous waves of fear and abomination that shook their immortal souls within. Hemortus heard the sound of Chief's low growl and looked over the pews behind him to see the small group of humans gasping and trembling in horror at the site of the enemy from Hell. Then a strange feeling of empathy and unity with the humans came over him, as he could see the terror that only he once knew and felt, was now also in their eyes and souls. Satan's sinister black eyes were so filled with the sins of revenge and hate, that one could barely see the ring of amethyst that faintly glowed around them. With his Staff of tarnished silver, he lunged at Allestra and violently swung his staff while uttering antiquated words of a dark language spoken before the dawn of man, hoping to knock her from the sacred altar. Allestra-Terra bounded through the air with unearthly force and raised her staff against Lucifer, hitting him squarely across his back as he turned to avoid it. Bolts of colored platinum sparks seared his scars of sin, causing him to cry out in anger and pain. Enraged by the first blow, he leaped at Allestra with supernatural agility as he swung his staff and aimed for her neck. As their staffs crossed, giant beams of goodness and evil clashed, sending spikes of crystal colors and crackling rods of silver and black, venting their awesome power throughout the cavern. Again, she raised her staff in self defense as Satan's weapon struck her wrist band and slightly grazed her arm sending a shock wave of sin to weaken her soul and Allestra winced in pain. Satan sneered with delight at the very thought of corrupting her soul, but the backlash of crystal power emitted from her wrist band, brought him the searing pain of goodness as the glowing crystals embedded themselves into his hand causing him even greater pain. Satan loudly cursed Allestra and viciously promised her a slow but sinful death in Hell, and the battle ensued as each sent counter-blows of agony to the other. Within his thoughts, his four demons spoke to him reminding him of the Reptile's failure, for time was running out and they would soon be cast from the Circle of Eternal Life. To succeed, he must strike her down quickly and seize the Waters of Creation, for this would destroy the Circle of Life and only then would he be the undisputed Master of Earth and it's Humanity. Allestra faithfully placed herself in God's hands as she concentrated and sent a message to Billy. "Communicate with the others and remind them to have faith and obey your words no matter what they may see or what I may openly say to them". Billy's heart raced as he quickly flashed Allestra's message through Sam's mind, and Byron knew from the look on Sam's face that the time had come, as Billy mentally repeated Allestra's message to the rest of them. Lucifer's voice echoed throughout the cavern;

"Warrior of God, thou who hast betrayed me, your time has come to feel the punishment of thy deed." Lucifer touched one of the hideous scars on his arm and a replica of the scar pulsated in his hands as he thrust it into the air, commanding it to attack Allestra. Allestra moved to avert the attack and raised her staff in defense, but it quickly embedded itself in her leg sending trailing scars representing the sins of jealousy, hatred, and pride throughout her right leg and upper thigh. The pain and agony she felt within her dropped Allestra to one knee as she fought to regain her defensive stance. Angella had tears in her eyes as she watched her beloved angel bend in pain and now she understood what evil could do to a person's heart and soul, for Angella's heart was pounding with great sorrow, but she kept telling herself to not lose faith as she drew upon the power within her. Visibly shaken, Allestra stumbled as she tried to regain herself, and she retaliated by sending out streams of purple rays from her glorious eyes toward the enemy. The agony he felt in his soul as the rays singed his body, enraged him even further as he duplicated other scars and savagely hurled them toward Allestra. The scars of sin attached themselves to her other leg, bringing with them the sins of lust, desire, and disobedience. The excruciating pain and burden of the sins tormented Allestra as she fell to the ground reeling from the cruel torture she felt deep within her soul. Satan sadistically smiled as he watched Allestra writher to the ground in pain, and then with great caution, he approached her and knew she was not yet totally helpless, for the crystal colors of goodness and light still emanated around her. As he stood above her, he gloated with thoughts of willful pride and gratification that she was no longer as powerful as he. For his moment of delicious revenge and unconditional terms had finally arrived, and he was at the brink of destiny's door by completely avenging himself and forcing her to give up the Holy Waters.

"Allestra, I command thee, Give me thy Holy Waters and I shall spare thy soul."

One could see the pain in her face as she looked at Satan and with all of her strength, she sent him her answer as she aimed the weakened rays from her deep purple eyes just missing the core of his chest and barely knocking him off balance. His eyes were ablaze with a burning fury as he lurched forward in an unbridled rage, but then stopped himself just short of attacking her and a cunning, devious smile crossed his scarred lips, for it was time to call upon Hemortus.

"Soul of Hemortus, I command thee to do my bidding".

The test had come and Hemortus could feel every inch of his tortured and captive soul pounding with unparalleled fear as Satan compelled Hemortus to come forth. The Dog Beast no longer growled as Hemortus rose from his crouched position and momentarily looked at Byron, Sam, and Lynn, as if to say he was truly sorry; and in their tearful eyes he thought he saw a glimmer of compassion and hope, for once he too was an innocent child of God, but had freely allowed himself to be led into Hell's grip of eternal damnation. Unable to gain the full strength of her legs, Allestra-Terra lay on the ground, still weakened by the deeds of sins that Satan had thrust upon her. As Hemortus approached Lucifer, Allestra seized the opportunity to remove one of her golden arm bands and sent a message to Billy.

"Byron and Sam must catch the golden band, for it will be protection against all harm."

Lucifer's nostrils flared open while his eyes darted from side to side, as only the words "all harm" faintly rushed by his mind; and he knew that Allestra was communicating with them. On his guard and unwilling to take any chances, Satan spoke only within the mind of Hemortus and again reminded Hemortus of eternal agony if he did not obey. Satan then turned from Hemortus and looked directly at the group of humans hiding behind the pews, sending Chills of terror through their minds and hearts. Complete fear was etched upon their faces as Angella held on to her grandmother and the Dog Beast sent out his warning growls. Screaming in fear and clutching her unborn child, Lynn cried out for help as the corrupt Archangel of evil and darkness swiftly raised her body in the air and pulled the unwilling human toward him. The group helplessly watched in shock as Byron stood on top of one of the pews waving his knife in his hand as he yelled out in defiance of Satan.

"Fight me, you worthless coward of scars, or are you afraid of a real man in the flesh."

"I've finally figured you out, Scarbag".

"You're nothing but a stink-weed now and You're sooooo ugly that nobody, not even God or Allestra can ever love you again, and that really hurts you, doesn't it Scarbag."

Satan's lips curled in anger for his eyes betrayed him as they revealed the truth in Byron's words, but Satan still would not let go of his captive as he spoke.

"After I destroy Allestra, it will give me great pleasure to fulfill thy wish to fight me, Brazen Human." Hemortus wretched in fear for Byron, but he also marveled in admiration at the character that Byron had shown by standing up to Satan, and this brought hope and courage to his soul.

Begging for herself and her child's life, Lynn stood beside Hemortus as the vortex of Hell opened and then Satan commanded Hemortus...

"Take the Yellow One, body and soul, into my domain, for I shall teach this human child my ways". Lynn screamed as she begged Hemortus with her pleading eyes to help her, but Hemortus could not bear to look at her as he turned to lead the way toward the opening of the vortex. Midway to the opening of hell's inferno, Hemortus clutched Lynn's hand and gazed toward Allestra, for he knew this was his moment of truth as he fought the terrified feelings within himself wondering if salvation could possibly be his. The Apollo of Dogs let out loud Savage Growls and jumped over the pews telling Satan that he was not afraid to attack him. As Satan turned his attention to Chief, Hemortus let go of Lynn's hand and told her ..,

"Run, Run for your life toward the others, Hurry, for your child's sake."

Satan became incensed with rage and sent out rays of black

and gray hoping to stop Lynn as she ran with all of the strength she had left within her. Allestra-Terra threw her golden band through the air and as Satan's evil rays were about to hit Lynn's body, sparks of gold from the holy band, hit and deflected them. Lynn kept running as Sam, Byron and the rest of the group urged her on while the bolts from Hell struck throughout the cavern. The holy band had now formed a larger circle as it loomed past Lynn while she desperately ran to catch up to it hoping to get within it's protection. Sam and Byron, with Frankie's help, stood on the pews just barely grasping the edge of the Golden Band as it almost soared past them. They braced themselves as the golden band grew larger in diameter and began encompassing the group and all of the people hidden in clusters within the cavern, radiating it's golden sparks of sanctuary. Lynn prayed to God to help her make it within the circle while Satan's killing rods struck through the cavern. Overwhelmed with exhaustion from the weight of her child, she stumbled and fell to the ground. Kartos and Sadessma left Satan's body to guard Allestra as he leaped through the cavern with the thought of taking the unborn human as his own for then Allestra would surely give up the Waters to save it's pitiful soul. Satan felt the thrill of murder pulse through the core of his pulsating scar as he slowly lowered his vile hand to touch Lynn's belly as she cowered in absolute horror; but the supernatural speed of the Yellow Diamond Comet entered Lynn's body just moments before Satan reached her, and Allestra of the Yellow Race whispered to Lynn's soul calming her fears with the promise that no harm would come to her or her unborn child. Allestra of the Yellow Race then formed her nimbus of yellow diamond crystals that radiated within and around Lynn, charring Satan's hand and wrist as he bent to touch her, for he could not penetrate the sparks of goodness and purity. Satan cursed as he violently withdrew his hand but then diabolically lowered his silver spear toward Lynn's belly, vowing to draw the unborn soul to him. Hemortus moved out from the shadows and courageously faced Satan

"You have taken many souls, but you shall not take an innocent child to your filthy bosom".

At first Satan sarcastically smirked, for he was surprised that the puny and detestable soul of Hemortus would dare to challenge he, Lucifer.

"And Hemortus, Are you going to stop me?", touted Satan.

Hemortus stared directly at Lucifer and in a stern voice, Hemortus again stood up to the beast from Hell. "Yes, I will stop thee for my soul is already lost and you cannot torment me any more than I am already". " So, I vow before GOD in Heaven that you will never take this innocent child and it will be the only good thing I have ever done, and I pray that maybe someday GOD will forgive me for all I have done wrong." Satan's sinister smile quickly faded from his lips at hearing GODs name, the ultimate betrayal uttered from the lips of a soul that was owned by him, and this sent Lucifer into a violent rage as he lunged toward Hemortus. In an instant, Chief grabbed Lynn's arm and pulled her through the golden protection of the Holy Circle while Satan seethed in a bath of fiery anger and his scars of sin swelled in size, as they savagely pulsated and split open displaying his uncontrollable wrath and fury at this final betrayal. With Hells' open Vortex directly behind him, Hemortus stood and faced man's greatest enemy.

"If there was time, I would claw thee now and the OTHER will not help thee for thy soul is still mine, and my army shall prepare thee for my tortures upon my victorious return, and thou shall suffer greatly as thy screams for mercy shall be heard throughout Hell's eternity".

Hemortus shouted "God's" name again as he lost his footing, for Satan sent a bolt of rays from his molten eyes to strike him into the Vortex. As Hermortus fell over the edge, Allestra of the Yellow Race threw a golden arm band through the closing hole of the Vortex,

"Catch it Hemortus, for it will protect thee."

Allestra of the Yellow Race then bolted through the cavern becoming the comet of yellow diamonds to re-enter Allestra-Terra's weakened silhouette. Satan leered at Allestra and viciously asked

"Besides the OTHER, Is it true that only an Archangel can touch the water.?"

Weak from the pain of sin, Allestra answered him truthfully for Satan already knew the answer and also knew Allestra could not lie.

"Lucifer asks me this question though he already knows the answer;

"Yes, this is true."

Lucifer then again demanded that Allestra give him the water.

"I shall punish thee until I get the Holy Waters",

as he thrust a replica of the sinful scar of Blasphemy upon her that sent more devastating and excruciating pain through her soul causing her to writher in agony as the soft glowing lights dimmed even more around her form, just barely sparkling as Allestra languished. Father Vincent and the Rabbi felt helpless, but they joined hands and continued praying, fervently believing that God would save them, as they and the rest of the group sadly watched the assault of evil on the pure Angel of the Lord. Angella closed her tear-filled eyes remembering what Allestra had taught her, and the little girl searched for God's power within her body and soul.

Knowing Allestra must tell the truth and hoping to trick her, Satan then asked

"Am I not Lucifer, Am I not still an Archangel"?

Allestra could barely speak for the torture and weight of his sins were excruciating to her and the pain in her voice echoed throughout the cavern as she began to answer the question.

"Lucifer, Is not a priest or any man of God, always a priest in the eyes of God, even though he may leave his flock, deny his sacred oath, or be defrocked?.."

Lucifer reveled in delight at hearing these words for she was actually telling him what he needed to know, which was no harm would come to him when he had the waters in his control because he was still an Archangel in God's eyes. He then commanded Allestra to

"Give me Thy Water, before I destroy thee completely."

Almost unconscious, Allestra just looked at him and did not respond, nor show any emotion to his demands as he again threatened her with the most damning and grave sin of all. From the core scar on his chest, Satan replicated the most brutal and horrible sin of all for it was the killing scar, the scar of MURDER. He held the mark of Cain above his head and as he readied himself to cast Allestra's soul into deeper agony, Angella rose to her feet holding Allestra's Staff of God's power within her hands and called Satan's name, knowing that seeing the staff would distract him from Allestra.

"If you destroy Allestra, you will never get the Water because I hold the key to the power that you seek." Satan's eyes glowed with evil as he cast his vision upon the golden circle and the little girl within it's protection, holding the power which he desperately needed. Even though his four generals warned him to be cautious, Satan moved toward Angella and then stopped midway before the Circle, for he dare not approach it too closely, as he could not stand its goodness and he thought to himself there must be a way to gain possession of the staff. Satan looked back at Allestra as she called out to Angella in a weakened voice.

"No Angella, do not give him the Staff for he will destroy Mankind."

Billy concentrated and within Angella's thoughts, he reminded her to listen to his words and Billy then told her and the rest of them what to do;

"The Races Must Unite as One".

Satan's nostrils instinctively flared open and his cunning eyes widened as he shrewdly searched for any signs of betrayal. Only the dead in hell could hear the terrified screams of his soul as Hemortus fell through Hell's bottomless pit drawing him closer to the epicenter of eternal pain and torture. As he dared to look down, the blackness began fading as he approached the inferno's mountains bathed in the blood and sludge of evil. His soul unwillingly gravitated toward the fire valley of Orr and he could see millions of souls moaning in agony as the punishment for their sins consumed and torched them as they cried out to Hemortus, "Betrayer", for they hoped Satan's torture of Hemortus would give them some relief from their own suffering. Hemortus frantically tried to break free of Hell's gravity hoping to grasp onto a fire rock or ledge as he saw the host of Satan's Legion of evil, once holy angels which became diabolical demons of sin in Lucifer's army, ready to rip and slash at his flesh to prepare him for Satan's return. As their claw-like talons reached for his soul, Hemortus again Called on "God" to help him. The powerful heavenly band sent out trails of golden gem dust and the legion of evil cowered in hatred and fear at the remembrance of Heaven, as the flecks of gem dust encircled Hemortus while the golden band wrapped itself around his right arm and lifted him out of their grasp and onto a smoldering ledge. Allestra's voice spoke to Hemortus as the soft whirlwind of golden flecks enraptured him in their goodness, for he would not be harmed by the evil below as long as he kept the golden band on his arm and waited faithfully upon the ledge. Hemortus bowed his head and wept as he still hoped he could truly redeem himself forever in God's eyes. Lucifer would now read Angella's mind before shrewdly striking a bargain with her, he thought, as he turned himself back into the handsome man with beautiful green eyes and looked toward Angella before speaking in a charming voice.

"How could he think we can be fooled like this"?, Sam shouted.

"He's acting like we haven't seen what he really is?", added Byron,

and the Dog Beast growled as Satan took two steps forward, then stopped and glared at Chief and looked at the detestable humans, wondering which one was the strongest in mind. In a sweet, charming voice, Satan deviously spoke.

"I could have hurt you that day in the cavern, Angella, but I did not, and I will not now." "Leave the circle, child, and I promise that I will not hurt you."

Felicia tugged at Angella,

"No Angella, Please, Please don't leave the protection of the

Circle."

Angella answered Satan

"No, Let Allestra come to us within the Circle, and I will give you the Staff of Power", replied Angella. As the little girl lowered the staff, Satan sent out purple and black rays to test her mind and search her soul, but as he tried to enter, he was so blinded by its purity and innocence, he could not tolerate the pain as he winced and trembled trying to hide his feelings of agony and of failure.

"If you come to me with the Staff, I will grant what you desire", stated Satan

as he continued to conceal the burning pain he felt in his soul. Still protected by the golden circle, Angella then temptingly raised the Staff above her head for Satan to see,

"There is one way for you to prove that you will let Allestra go."

"And What is that, sweet Angella, asked Satan."

Angella spoke boldly defying Satan

"If you are telling the truth, then prove it by bowing down to GOD, Creator of All, and beg HIM for forgiveness." "Only then, Will I give you the Staff of Truth and Power."

Satan let out a blood-curdling scream of diabolical madness as he turned back into the terrifying demon he really was and he cursed Angella.

"Blasphemer, human bitch of innocence, I shall slay thee and all that thy hold precious."

"I promise thee, that I shall torture thy Sweet Allestra until she bows down to me if you do not give me thy Key to the Waters." "Dost thou think that the Divine Circle will protect thee forever?, for Thou art human and will need food and water even within the protection of thy Circle".

The people in the cavern prayed and cried for God's help as Satan bounded toward Allestra with total revenge seething in his eyes, as his scars pulsated larger and split open with a rage of vengeance and fury that he felt deep within his sin-laden soul. Together with Sam and Byron, Angella stepped through the sparks of protection and yelled to Satan. Allestra raised her weakened arm telling Angella

"Angella, Do not give the demon my staff, for it will mean doom and darkness to the whole earth."

Billy's voice then boomed through the air.

"We must save Allestra, give the Staff to Satan and hope he will let Allestra Go Free."

Angella hesitated but finally handed the Staff to Byron as Lucifer turned toward them and watched in anticipation, keeping his eyes on the Holy Staff at all times. As Satan headed toward Byron, Byron flipped the staff to Sam and said

"Apache Warrior, Throw the arrow true and straight, just as God's Holy Warrior would do."

Sam paused for a moment and looked at Byron in friendship, and then with great power, he thrust the mighty staff as far and as high as he could, aiming it to the other side of the Cavern where Allestra lay weakened, for the crystal lights around her were so dim by now, that they were sure she was very close to the end of her valiant struggle against the enemy. After Sam threw the mighty pointed staff, the three of them scurried back under the protection of the golden nimbus while all in the cavern witnessed the Holy Staff sail through the air as its glowing crystal spewed out streams of white lightning that bounced off the walls of the cavern. Satan leaped in mid-air and in his scar-covered hands, he at last snared the power he had been seeking for so long. Overjoyed, his four generals hastily reveled in their victory, begging to finish off Allestra and enslave the humans, but Satan first wanted the water, for time was running out and as he looked at Allestra's body, he knew she was no longer a threat to him and there would be an eternity to quench his thirst of evil desires. Satan seemed beguiled by the staff and its majestic crystal, for it brought back memories as he momentarily flinched at the feel of it in his hands, and then an unholy smile slowly crossed his lips as he remembered how to use it. The Crystal changed from the Star Ruby to the Emerald, from the Emerald to the Yellow Diamond, from the Yellow Diamond to the Sapphire, but when it changed to the Holy Amethyst, Satan knew he had found the key to unleash the Waters of Creation into his power, for he would now truly be the Master of Humanity. Lucifer pointed the deep amethyst crystal toward the ground of the Cavern invoking the waters to come forth. The ground ruptured and shook as it gave way to geysers of deep purple streams of water that magnificently shot up into the air throughout the cavern and large pools of heaving and swirling purple and blue water sprang up before his eyes. An amethyst and blue frothy mist rose from the pools of water as they gathered and inter-locked with each other, forming a river of rapids surrounding Allestra, Satan, and his generals. As Satan stood on holy ground, he admired the majesty and could feel the ultimate power that only the Waters of Creation could bring him, except for one last deed to make the Waters completely his. He walked with Great Pride toward the flowing water, for he was still the One and Only most powerful Archangel and Ruler of Hell's eternity, and now he would prove it. As Satan bent down beside the waters, he slowly moved his hand to within an inch of touching them when he heard Angella's voice. Satan looked up to see the dog, Chief, and the four young races of mankind on the other side of the river's bank, unprotected by the Circle of Goodness. Angella's words of

"Unite against the Enemy",

echoed through the cavern, as Sam, Byron, and Lynn stood beside her. Billy's words then reverberated throughout the cavern as he called to the people to unite against the evil before them. Joe and Sara along with Felicia, Father Vincent, and Rabbi Silverman stood and raised their voices repeating the words "Unite against the Enemy".

As more of the people stood, their voices joined in the refrain until all of the colors of mankind had but one voice. Satan watched in disbelief as he listened with contempt at their brazen but feeble attempt to stop him. The colors of mankind became one unified voice as they repeated

"Unite against the Enemy".

As Satan's generals leered at the people, Satan raised his head and in a sinister tone.

"I have defeated your Holy Warrior and you dare to defy me." "I will not let lowly humans trick me from taking what is mine and I shall remember this day, for Mankind shall beg for a mercy that will never come."

With unparalleled quickness, he forcefully plunged his vile hand into the Waters of Creation as a willful and spiteful smile of great power and satisfaction crossed his sin-filled face. As he reveled in the sweetness of his power, Satan slowly began to remove his hand from the swirling waters. His smile began to fade and his deep set eyes glared as they moved from side to side expressing an unknown fear of what he was suddenly beginning to feel. Just as he lifted his hand from the water, the blue and purple liquid coursed through his body and turned his scars of sin into nerve-ending fibers of pain, as the waters traveled within him and slowly made their way toward the very core of his evil. Seizures of silvery blue lightning emanated from his left hand, sucking his powerless generals into his body as Satan cursed in agony, for the holy fluid became a molten liquid of Mercury that began to attack the central scar of his sins, and his soul began to weaken at being caught in the grip of the Almighty's wrath. Even though he was seriously wounded, Satan still had enough supernatural power with which to avenge himself and so he cunningly bounded over the river and fixed his sinister gaze upon Angella who would be his victim of partial retribution. Allestra-Terra slowly dragged herself toward the river's edge and placed her hand into the Holy waters as her life-force rejuvenated and the crystal lights again glowed and sparkled ever so brightly around her. She then raised her body to it's ultimate apex of power and glory as she called upon the sacred Sword of Crucis and dipped it into the Holy Waters. As she withdrew the annoited Sword, it radiated with God's magnificent and consuming flames of orange and red fire-opals. Byron and Sam frantically tried to release Angella, but her legs would not move as Satan's mind had willed her body paralyzed, and Felicia screamed in horror as she watched Angella helplessly caught in Satan's evil vice. As hard as they tried, Byron and Sam could not free her, and just before Satan could reach them, Chief courageously leaped into the air as he attacked the greatest enemy the World has ever known, but Satan easily fended off the great dog and threw him aside. As the boiling fluid of Mercury quickened through his veins, Satan grew weaker and he knew that he must quickly posess Angella's body and soul if he were to sustain himself and reap revenge at any cost, against the Creator. Praying for God's help, Angella closed her eyes as tears streamed down her face, while her lips and body quivered with a grave and heightened fear at the thought of Satan's touch being within an inch of her body and soul. In a cruel voice, he spoke as he extended his hand to touch the locks of blonde hair on her head, "No longer shall thou be innocent of heart and soul, for I shall give thee all of the gifts I once bestowed upon thy ancestors, and thy soul shall be mine forever". Satan voice sounded like that of an unknown beast, wounded and in agony, as he half-way dropped to his knees in torment. As he unwillingly fell to the ground, he raised his eyes to see Allestra-Terra's face, as she then branded his chest with the Mighty Sword of Crucis that compelled him to drop in total submission. Satan moaned in anguish at the excruciating torment he felt deep within his evil soul, for the streaming fire opals of the sacred Sword intermingled with the molten Mercury fluid of the Waters, causing Satan even greater pain and fear, thus enforcing God's power to remind Lucifer that Dominus would no longer tolerate the evil wrought against Mankind. As he lay on holy ground, bolts of molten mercury burst through his hands and feet and began encasing his body in a cocoon of supernatural quicksilver fire and pain. The people slowly came out of their hiding places to join Angella and the others as they watched the unmatched power of God's Hand at work before them in reverence and awe. His voice reflected the viscious hatred harbored in his soul as he cursed Allestra and spoke with great malice toward Allestra.

"Warrior of the OTHER, Thou shall pay dearly for thy betrayal and I vow that I shall destroy all that you love and protect unto their generations, for Thou has lied to me."

Allestra answered him as the silvery liquid quickly surged into the scars of his neck steadfastly moving upward toward the scars on his face.

"God created his most beloved and favored Archangel Lucifer whose special power and light was but one tenth of an eon below that of Dominus, because he so loved Lucifer". "Thy pride and evil has made thee Satan, no longer an Angel of Beauty and Light, but a beast of Darkness, deceit, and vile corruption". "Yet, in HIS eyes, thou were created by HIS Hand as an Archangel of the Tenth Power in his first house, and so therefore Thou shall not yet die but thou shall feel the great punishment and pain of thy own evil that thou has wrought upon all created by the hand of Dominus". "Until the passing of one Tri-eon, no longer shall thou destroy nature, No longer shall thou hurt and kill the creatures of the earth, and No longer will thou be allowed to walk the earth stalking the Children of Colors to set them against each other, for the Gates of the lower Vortex will soon be sealed and no more souls shall be taken by thee."

Before their eyes, Hell's Vortex opened and readied itself to receive Satan into its bottomless depth once more. In the ancient language of her kind, Allestra called upon the soul of Hemortus to come forth out of the darkness. Upon hearing her words, Satan vehemently blasphemed as he cursed in anger.

"You dare to break the Seal and Boundary of the Covenant"?, he cried out.

"His soul has already entered and it is sealed within the Claim, for it is bound to me by the Dimension of it's Deeds".

Hemortus made his way through the molten mist of the Vortex and once again stepped into the Earth's plane. His eyes shined at the site of Allestra for he felt a loving force within him, and in an instant he knew he had a heart for it now beat with new life and the hope of redemption. Satan closed his eyes and willed Hemortus to obey as Satan demanded Hemortus help set he and his demons free. Hemortus closed his mind, heart, and soul to Satan, proving he would no longer obey him, as he stood close to Allestra-Terra with tears of joy welling up in his eyes.

"Only Dominus has the power and the right as Creator and God to rejudge any Soul that has still a speck of his light, and so thus, He commands the right of re-judgement over the soul of Hemortus", said Allestra. Satan's war-cry of evil resounded through the cavern and filtered into the Inferno as moans of millions of captive souls in hell were heard; for in an earth's moment, the cocoon of Mercury and pain would soon imprison his power over humanity. Satan opened his wild eyes which were black as sin and that now contained silver quivering flames of the Mercury's fire within. The Sarcophagus of evil then lifted upward into the air as it swirled through the Vortex of Hell as Satan cursed Allestra and Hemortus, for the Gates of Hell would soon be sealed.

"I shall remember Thy betrayal and before the Tri-eon ends, there shall be a new dawn for me as I shall regain thy soul, Hemortus, and the souls of the future generations of the four despised races". "Heed My words, for by my oath, I shall see thee in Hell, Allestra, for we shall battle again and I will destroy all that thou has nurtured and all humans who love thee and thy kind".

CHAPTER 7

Allestra stood upon the mound of Holy Ground with the four Archangels of color beside her, as the swirling river flowed more gently around them. Hemortus sat beside the waters and his heart beat with happiness as he watched the people that were now beginning to gather on the other side of its banks, while Allestra cleansed her Holy Staff of Power and Light in God's River. When she was finished, she turned to face the people.

"Within the hour, the earth shall be restored of it's life and so shall Mankind's life be restored; but, before Dominus turns them into Earth's waters, there is one more thing left he wishes to do."

The four archangels of colors stood beside Allestra as she called upon Byron to approach her, and the Black Allestra moved a few steps forward and held out her hand motioning him to come forward.

"Son of the Black Race, through the waters of Creation, thou shall come forward to me".

Byron looked at the others as he heard her words and then unafraid he stepped into the River of Life and walked through them until he reached the mound of Holy Ground and stood before Allestra. The Great Archangel withdrew a beautiful Midnight Blue Sapphire from her arm band and placed it in Byron's hand. "This is the Stone of Wisdom to be passed down to those of your calling, and in the years to come, you shall be a great leader and the people will honor and respect your judgement and wisdom, as you shall stand for justice and unity for all of the colors of mankind."

Byron was speechless as he silently looked upon the exquisite face of Allestra and he could feel the love and warmth of her smile that would never leave his soul, as he accepted her beautiful gift. Allestra then raised her Holy Staff in the air and called Sam's name.

"Son of the Red Race, come and walk through the Waters of Creation and Join thy brother."

The young Apache Warrior put his feet into the Holy river and felt the healing touch of God's glorious power surge within him as he approached Allestra.

"Beloved Son of the Red Race, thy destiny awaits thee for thy Race has always protected and honored the mother Earth and its wondrous creatures." "God has bestoyed upon thee the gifts of vision, sensitivity, and the great power of healing, for you shall be the first New Healer of the earth and of it's creatures entrusted to you and those that shall follow".

"Behold the Glorious Stone entrusted to thee"..............

and then Allestra placed a magnificent Deep, Green Emerald into the palm of his hand. Sam's heart pounded with joy as he accepted Allestra's gift, and as Byron turned to hug his beloved friend, he could see that Sam's face was smooth and handsome, and no longer paralyzed. God's Warrior then called upon the "Daughter of the Yellow Race to come to her." When Lynn reached the other side of the River, Allestra of the Yellow Race grasped Lynn's hand and led her to Allestra-Terra.

"Daughter of the Yellow Race, God loves you for the humility, faith, and patience you have shown, for you posess the loving capacity of forgivness toward others who have maligned, hated, and shunned you because of your color."

Allestra than handed her the most brilliant Yellow Diamond ever created.

"Your child shall be the first born onto this New and Free Earth and he shall shine as this yellow diamond, for he and the diamond will be a strong beacon of golden light and energy to all of the Roses within the garden of eternal life, and he and his children will align themselves with the others on the the path to glory against all evil".

Angella's laughter-filled eyes were as large as life, as Allestra-

Terra called her name.

"Beloved and pure child of the White Race, walk through the Waters of Dominus and take thy place beside me once more."

Allestra-Terra walked toward the edge of the Holy Waters to greet Angella and then bent down beside the precious little girl with the golden locks of hair and adorable dimples. From her right arm band, Allestra drew out the most majestic and powerful Star Ruby ever created by God and placed it Angella's hand.

"I give thee the stone of great Power, truth, and Affection for it will protect thee and the races for all of eternity."

Allestra-of the White Race then handed God's Book to Allestra-Terra as she again spoke to Angella. "The Sacred Book of knowledge and law is in your hands to record and preserve for all of the generations unto the Tri-Eon, for you will be the great mentor and teacher of truth to all of the Races and they will turn to thee for your honesty, truth, and the strength you carry within, for only those who are innocent and pure of heart may be keeper of the Sacred Book".

Allestra then gently kissed Angella on her forehead and Angella wrapped her arms around the great angel, knowing this would be the last time they would be together and she would cherish this memory forever in her mind and heart. Allestra then rose to her feet and called to Father Vincent and Felicia to walk through the holy waters of faith. From her wrist band of God's gems, Allestra-Terra gave Felicia a large oval milky moonstone, for this personified Felicia's loving memories of God's creations.

"By the end of this day, the moon shall rise again and take its rightful place in Earth's sky and your memories will be complete, my lovely Felicia; for you have given Angella your knowledge, your love, and beautiful memories of her own to cherish and keep."

From the river, Allestra then filled a waxen flask with the precious Holy Waters and sealed it as she faced Father Vincent.

"Vincent, Priest of Dominus, you proved your faith as you protected His Holy Chalice against the touch of evil that stood upon the Blessed Altar of Life, and thou has loved and respected all of the faiths of Mankind. Before I release the waters, the Lord gives you the honor to protect this Holy Water in God's temple". "It must be safe-guarded for the future generations of mankind, for evil will come again".

Vincent bowed his head in reverence and love as he accepted the challenge of the powerful Gift that God had bestoyed upon him and he thanked God, for his heart could feel his power and glory within. Not thinking of himself, Billy sat in his wheelchair as he watched in amazement along with the others, at the splendor of God's Holy Warrior before them. He was happy that Sam was his son and he wished that his wife could be there to see how Sam had grown in mind and body. Then the voice filled his mind for all to hear.

"Billy, thou who are the most strong in mind, in hope, and in thy unshakable faith".

Billy quickly looked up as he heard Allestra's unmistakable voice, and he and everyone could see her as she walked into the river and stopped at midpoint.

"Billy, dost thou believe in the power of God?".

"Yes, You know I do, answered Billy."

Allestra then gloriously called upon Billy again to

"Rise from thy chair and meet me in God's Glorious Waters".

Billy was shocked as he momentarily hesitated, but then forced himself out of his wheelchair as he shakily stood and held on to its side arms. He then thought to himself,

"I am an Apache Warrior and God will give me the strength for what I yearn to do."

Allestra raised her hand upward and smiled as she spoke

"That is enough, I shall come to thee as you came to me and had faith that very day in the Temple of God"

Allestra moved toward Billy and as she drew close to him, she poured the holy water from the river onto his body and legs, and Billy could barely contain his emotion as he and Allestra walked through the river to join the others on Holy Ground. Allestra then gave Billy the Stone of Faith, The Holy Amethyst, which was as deep and radiant as the color of her divine eyes, and the people cheered with joy and happiness at what they had seen.

"I have not forgotten thee, Oh, Loyal one; and Allestra then summoned the

"Apollo of Dogs", "Noble and Loyal Creature of God" "I call upon you who have protected and loved mankind with thy loyalty through the ages."

Chief swiftly bounded into the river, bouncing and splashing with excitement at the mention of his name and in a moment, he stood at Allestra's side as she soothing spoke to him. From her wrist band, she gathered the most exquisite garnet ever created and hung it around the elegant dog's neck.

"This is the stone that guided the arc and made it safe for all of the creatures held in its cargo."

"This is the stone symbol for all creatures created by God, and this is the stone of thy courage and power, Great Apollo of Dogs"., "for this stone is also the Eagle's, it is also the Lion, it is also the bear and the horse, as it is for all the creatures of the earth".

As Chief licked her hand, he looked into her beautiful eyes and he knew that soon she would be leaving this earthly place.

"Go Chief, Take thy honored place by your master's side, for Sam has always respected and loved all of the creatures of the earth, and there will be a new beginning and a new bond between creature and human kind, never to be cruelly treated or hunted again".

The four Archangels then entered Allestra's body as she prepared herself to set the water's free. She raised her Staff toward the heavens commanding the clouds to return as the Powerful White Crystal Diamond sent large bolts of white, purified lightning into the skies as they began reflecting the glow of a beautiful red-dusk, for the sun was being pulled back into its rightful axis by the Hand of God. The people looked up toward the skies and Felicia once again felt the kiss of a gentle cool breeze touch her skin as the planet, Mars, gave up the Earth's moon which now softly glowed in full bloom as it cast its silvery face upon the earth once more. As they looked upward, the people wept with happiness and thanks as millions of stars again filled the skies above with twinkling bursts of starlight. As Allestra-Terra pointed the Great Amethyst Crystal toward the Waters, she invoked God's power.

"Against all evil, I have protected thy great power of Creation since the dawns of thy eternity, and now My Great Lord, it is with your wish and your power, that I now set thy Waters of Creation free to rejuvenate the earth, it's creatures, and thy beloved humanity." "I thank thee for thy great honor that thou has bestoyed upon me, and soon I shall return to my beloved home to again stand by thy side in thy glory and love."

The brilliance of the Crystal Amethyst cast it's shadow on the frothy waters as they flowed upward, forming several large Geysers of magnificence and splendor continuing to spiral higher into the sky and then planted their seeds within the giant clouds above. After the last Geyser was gone, Allestra turned to the people and told them that soon a Heavenly rain would fall and replenish the earth and her waters for all of the creatures and mankind. She also warned them that from this day foreward, everyone should honor, respect, and live in harmony and peace with each other as well as all of God's creatures. Allestra reminded them that God adored the little children and that any violent act commited against an innocent child, would be dealt with great harshness by the Hand of God. Allestra-Terra then looked toward Hemoratus and he knew that soon they would be leaving this life, and his heart pounded anxiously for the time was close at hand for his rejudgement. Tears of sadness and joy rolled down Angella's face as she suddenly ran toward Allestra to hug her just one more time. As The Great Angel knealt down to hug the little girl goodbye, two majestic pearl white wings that only Angella could see and feel, gently enveloped her in a protected, but yet warm and gentle hug as Allestra-Terra lovingly looked into the little girl's eyes.

"Sweet little angel, remember what I have taught you, for you and the others must teach and hand down the power and knowledge to the future generations." "I tell thee now of a great secret to be kept as a bond between us, for Dominus has chosen thee because of thy innocent and spotless soul". "At the end of God's Tri-Eon, Satan will walk the earth one last time, but he will be defeated when our secret meets with the colors of mankind and the stones become as the crystal, for there is another race of thy kind that are without sin". As Allestra looked into Angella's eyes, she then silently spoke within Angella's mind, divulging more of the great power of the secret to the little girl. After Allestra was done, she then told Angella,

"I will always love and watch over you, so do not be afraid, for you will never be alone and we shall meet again". Angella gazed into Allestra's magnetic eyes as she extended her hand to touch the face of her beloved Archangel one last time. In all of her magnificent power, Allestra-Terra then stood and looked into the faces of the colors of mankind before her. In a human instant, one shattering hue of an electric-like flash lit the sky as far as ones eyes could see, and Allestra and Hemortus were gone. The great Eagle arched his neck and blinked his eyes as he fixed his site on the attractive glow of the soft flames below. The amber flames of the friendly campfires cast their reflection on the shore of Lake Erie, for many of the people had gathered in cozy clusters around them, and they talked about what had happened and what the future would hold. Billy had salvaged the Statue of Allestra-Terra and placed it beside their campfire as he lovingly worked to inscribe Allestra-Terra's name on its base. While he diligently worked on the statue, Father Vincent, Rabbi Silverman, and Joe visited each campfire and eagerly made plans with everyone to help in rebuilding their lives and homes together. Chief playfully rolled over and nudged Sam, while Frankie listened intently to Sam and Byron's story of Allestra-Terra and their great journey to find the Yellow One. Angella's thoughts were on Allestra and of how much she missed her, but when she looked at Lynn to see that she was now comfortably asleep; Angella's eyes twinkled with happiness as a smile crossed her lips, for Sara was humming a soft lullabye while she rocked Lynn's newborne baby in her arms. Felicia walked toward the edge of the Lake and gazed at the reborn rippling waters glistening from the glow of

Earth's silvery moon, and the golden campfires which brought Felicia new memories to cherish for the rest of her life. As she looked at the moon and the stars, their images lingered in her eyes and she thanked God for giving back the World these glorious memories which she had feared would be lost forever. A feeling of profound understanding and release came over her, as her whole being was filled with complete belief and hope that all races would finally live together in peace and harmony. Only then, could they respect, love, and cherish God's nature that was created for all of mankind; giving their children the most blessed gifts of truly loving and precious memories from this moment on. Felicia's heart beat with gladness as she raised her eyes to the Heavens and felt a gentle rain falling on her face, for she knew then that winter would also come and no longer would the cool kiss of snow be just a forgotten memory. Angella walked toward her grandmother and slid her fingers into Felicia's comfortable and warm hand...

"Grand mama, You know....Allestra really does have wings"

A large smile crossed Felicia's lips as tears of happiness gently welled in her eyes, and she tenderly squeezed her grand-daughter's hand;

"Yes, Angella, she does have wings and they're as perfect as Winter's first windbown snowflake".